*Thorsby*

*BY THE SAME AUTHOR*

All Kinds of Courage
For All Good Men
Little Maid All Unwary
Sybilla

# THORSBY

## Joan Hessayon

CENTURY
LONDON MELBOURNE AUCKLAND JOHANNESBURG

Copyright © Joan Hessayon 1988
*All rights reserved*
First published in Great Britain in 1988 by
Century Hutchinson Ltd
Brookmount House, 62–65 Chandos Place
London WC2N 4NW

Century Hutchinson South Africa (Pty( Ltd
PO Box 337, Bergvlei, 2012 South Africa

Century Hutchinson Australia Pty Ltd
PO Box 496, 16–22 Church Street, Hawthorn
Victoria 3122, Australia

Century Hutchinson New Zealand Ltd
PO Box 40–086, Glenfield, Auckland 10
New Zealand

ISBN 0 7126 1828 7

Photoset by Deltatype Ltd, Ellesmere Port
Printed and bound in Great Britain by
Anchor Brendon Ltd, Tiptree, Essex

*This book is dedicated to my first grandson,
Alexander James Gibbs*

# Chapter One

My Uncle Marcus was an ugly man, even when wearing his finest clothes and a smile. Unfortunately, he was wearing neither when he burst into the parlour of the Royal Oak Inn on a bitterly cold day last January. The wind had whipped his fat cheeks to a high colour and his caped coat flapped open as he stalked towards me. He was in a rage, but his groom, a wizened little man in his sixties, wore a malicious grin.

I jumped to my feet and backed a few paces closer to the fire. 'Uncle, I can explain –'

'You have no need to explain, Elinor. I know everything. You climbed out of a window at the Hertfordshire convent to which I had sent you because of your persistent misconduct, and then you walked for two days to reach this inn in Essex to join your lover. What is there to explain?'

'I couldn't bear Mother Theresa, Uncle Marcus. It was unfair of you to send me to Hertfordshire.' He took a pace nearer and I shrank back. 'Don't take me away just yet, I beg of you. Tad is out with some of his friends, but has promised me that he will return soon. Let me at least say farewell to him. He will be very worried if he returns to find me gone.'

'Worried?' laughed my uncle. 'Do you think the gallant captain cares about you? Eight hundred pounds a year, fifty acres of prime farmland and a tidy manor house in Gloucestershire. That's what the captain cares about, and he shan't get his hands on them.'

'He loves me for myself, not my fortune.'

Uncle Marcus turned to the groom and winked broadly. 'My niece says the captain loves her for herself.

I think she must be mad, don't you?' They both laughed uproariously.

'It's madness right enough,' said Dobson, slapping one of his short muscular thighs. He had been a jockey in his youth, and his skin was like leather from a lifetime spent out of doors. 'Oh, Mr Burns-Roberts, I do believe you have hit the nail on the head. Oh, sir, what wit! Miss must be *mad* to think the captain loves her.'

My uncle took me by the arm and pulled me into the middle of the room. It occurred to me that I was not putting up a very spirited fight to stay with the man I loved, but I couldn't seem to rouse myself from the shock of seeing my Uncle Marcus walk into the room.

He turned his head slightly, to speak to the groom. 'The landlord's wife is packing my niece's belongings. Hurry her along, Dobson. Tie the box on to the back of the carriage as quickly as you can. We've still a way to travel. But bring me the girl's cape. It's perishing cold today and we wouldn't want her to freeze to death, now would we?'

They all came out to watch my ignominious departure on that raw day – the landlord and his sneering wife, the pot boys and maids, even two of the local farmers, still holding their tankards of ale. My disgrace was their peep show. No one spoke to me; no one said goodbye or called my uncle to account for handling me so roughly as he all but threw me into the carriage. We were away from the Royal Oak within a couple of minutes.

The closed carriage was cold and, since it was going at such a rattling pace, uncomfortable. My uncle had a lap rug which he kept for his own comfort while I clung to the strap and shivered. So I was somewhat startled when he produced his hip-flask and handed it to me even before taking a swig himself.

'You've had a bit of a shock, Elinor,' he said conversationally. 'Better fortify yourself against the cold.'

I don't care for spirits, and had tasted brandy only once in my life, on the day my mother died. On this day, however, I didn't hesitate. There was scarcely a mouthful left in the flask, but what there was burned all the way down.

'I'm sorry, Uncle. I seem to have drunk it all.'

'No matter,' he said with a slight laugh and, putting the flask back in his large coat pocket, turned his face to the window and didn't speak again.

I very soon understood the reason for his amusement – the brandy had been heavily laced with opium. I was sucked down into a world of nightmares, terrifying images and a sense of total helplessness. I knew I should be afraid, that I was in danger, yet I knew also that I was powerless to save myself.

'Where are we going?' I managed to ask. 'Why?'

'East,' I heard my uncle reply as if from a great distance. 'Somewhere safe from the captain and any other man who might have his eye on your fortune. You've been a burden to me over the years, Elinor. *Open your eyes!* Can you hear me?'

I opened my eyes with considerable effort, saw my uncle in a blur, and closed them again as he carried on talking. 'I didn't mind too much when you came to live with me. Your father was my favourite brother, after all. Now they are all dead: Harry and Alfred before ever they reached manhood, then Josiah when you were still a lass. You are my only living relative. I did my duty. But matters have changed, haven't they? You've grown up and become a damnable nuisance and I, well, I have run into a spot of bother. The law is hard, my girl. I must pay the money back. I could hang. Can't have that. What would your aunt do then? You owe me a debt of gratitude for having taken you in when your parents died. You have cost me a pretty penny. What I am doing is only fair. My conscience is clear.'

I was incapable of answering, or even of fully comprehending what he was saying, but I was to have many months of enforced inactivity in which to puzzle out my uncle's last words to me, in which to consider the enormity of his betrayal.

I did not wake again for some hours and when I did it was to find myself in a small room containing nothing but a bed and a night table. There was not even a window. The only air entering the room came from a small grille set in the door and it didn't take me long to find out that the door was locked. I thought at first that I was in prison and it was several days before I discovered that I had been committed to a madhouse. Of course, I screamed to be set free; shouted to the owner, Mr McCann, that I was as sane as anyone. Nevertheless, within a fortnight he had brought me to doubt it. I sank into apathy and longed for the release of death.

Ironically, I had no idea then how fortunate I was. Apparently, I was a private patient. My uncle (acting, I'm sure from a guilty conscience) paid fifteen shillings a week for my board, which was why I had a room of my own and was allowed to take my meals with the McCanns.

Then one day, less than a month after my arrival, Mr McCann informed me that my uncle had died and my aunt was not willing to continue to pay for my privileges. She would subscribe just seven shillings and sixpence a week to ensure that I was locked away for ever. So I was moved to the attic, to sleep with those who were raving mad, incontinent and occasionally violent. It was only after one of them had attacked me in the night, that I was once more allowed to sleep in my little cell. But as a pauper I was still forced to eat the slops that were served to the pauper lunatics. Now denied all reading matter, most of my privacy and what remained of my self-respect, I fought to keep my sanity and to hold on to dreams of rescue.

And so the days passed, without variation, stimulus or

hope, until one day when I was standing by the window of what Mr McCann was pleased to call 'the women's day room'. The sunlight had been sliced into neat squares by the grillework of the window and lay, slightly distorted, on the warped floorboards of this musty, mould-brown cupboard of a room. The window was open, so I knew it was warm outside. I thought it must be the month of May, for the trees were in leaf and horse chestnuts, too far away to be seen clearly, glowed with white candles of flowers. I thought I had calculated the time since January the twenty-second with tolerable accuracy. It *must* be May, but the exact day was unfortunately beyond me. I knew the year, of course – 1813. I would never forget the year. On January the twenty-second, 1813, Elinor Burns-Roberts had been buried alive by her own uncle.

As I looked out of the window, what I saw set my heart racing, turned my knees to water and forced me, at last, to examine my courage. A visitor was arriving! The first carriage ever to travel up the long drive in full daylight, at least since I descended into this hell on earth, was standing at the front door at this moment. I saw a passenger alight as I pressed my face against the grille which covered the window. I had no idea who the man was nor why he had come, but I prayed he would bring me salvation today. Or else there would be no salvation for me at all.

For weeks I had dreamed of this moment, planning just what I would do and say. Now I wondered if I dared. What would happen to me if I failed to convince him of my story? Paradoxically, I wished he would go away, come again the next day after I had prepared myself mentally for this important moment. My mind was sluggish and I was desperately afraid that I would not be able to speak at all.

Footsteps in the corridor some ten minutes later set me shaking. I heard voices outside the door. Mr

McCann was whining, supplicating in a manner I had never heard before. The same Mr McCann who had in the past fixed his eye on me and by the terrible force of his personality reduced me to quivering obedience.

'Mr Flemynge, sir,' Mr McCann was saying. 'I don't understand your displeasure, I don't really. I got me a proper licence. We've never had no complaints in ten years, I assure you. None whatsoever. Mr Harding, the magistrate what was the visitor before you, he never came but once every three or four years and then he never stayed above ten minutes. Just signed the visitors' book and went about his business.'

'What is this room?' enquired a deep voice.

So near! I put a steadying hand against the wall, willing the visitor to step inside, yet afraid of the outcome if he did.

'That's the women's day room,' said Mr McCann. 'No need to see it. You don't want to go in there. It's just like the men's day room and you've already seen that.'

'Nevertheless –'

A key was turned, the door opened and the visitor entered, closely followed by Mr McCann, his ratlike face contorted with worry.

My first impression of the visitor was one of splendour – a tall man of about thirty, wearing a fine blue riding coat, tight buff breeches and bright new Hessians. Then I noticed the gauntness of his face, all nose and chin, the hard eyes taking in every detail. He seemed displeased with what he saw, as well he might be: five females in varying states of health crammed into one sparsely furnished room no more than five paces square. His roving eye fell on me, and I knew I must speak now.

'Please, sir. My name is Elinor Burns-Roberts. I will be twenty-one years old on the twenty-ninth of May and I don't belong here. *I am not a lunatic.*'

The visitor looked at me with narrowed eyes and I strained to return his gaze calmly, to show by my expression and demeanour that I was indeed sane. This was no easy task. In the months I had been locked away, I had learned all the expressions of madness and no doubt added a few of my own – certainly the look of black despair, perhaps even of stupidity. Lethargy had overtaken me in these months, a slowing down of mind and emotions. I wanted the stranger to see that I was different from the other women, but a smile of quick-witted optimism eluded me. My situation was so desperate that I was paralysed by the fear of failure to gain this man's sympathy.

'Mr Flemynge,' Mr McCann said. 'Some of the women are raving, your typical dangerous lunatics. Others just have nonsensical ideas. Now this poor object –'

'Object?' said the visitor coldly.

'Object of pity, sir. This poor deranged object of pity believes her wicked aunt and uncle had her committed so's he could make free with her fortune. That's a common delusion, that is. I blame them novels that young women read. Anyways, her uncle is dead.'

'He did!' I cried. 'I have a small fortune and a manor house in Gloucestershire. As God is my witness, sir, it is the truth. I was brought here on January the twenty-second –'

The visitor turned to Mr McCann, lifting one dark eyebrow in mute enquiry, and McCann scratched his ear thoughtfully.

'I'm that disappointed, sir. I felt certain that we were effecting a cure with this young object. When she was brought to us, she had no control over herself at all.'

'What is the date today?' the visitor asked sharply. I flinched, aware of the danger in hesitation, yet unable to answer either quickly or sensibly.

'I'm . . . I'm not sure. I've tried to keep track of the time as best I can, but you know how it is when one receives a terrible shock . . . or no, I don't suppose you do. Anyway, at first I didn't think about anything except . . . ' I rubbed my forehead. 'It is now May, I'm sure of that.'

'Yes,' said the visitor. 'It is May. And what county are we in?'

'I don't know, but it's not my fault. There is nothing wrong with my reasoning. I know that this place is called Chennings. It's just that no one ever said. Or . . . yes –' I swallowed a growing lump in my throat and took a desperate chance that my uncle had told me the truth. 'Suffolk?'

'We are in Essex, just a few miles from Chelmsford.' He smiled dismissively. 'I am sorry, my dear.'

He began to move away. In desperation I clutched at his sleeve. 'Please sir, I beg of you. Your questions are no test of my sanity. Do something about this terrible injustice. I don't belong here!'

The visitor looked down at my hand on his sleeve, then up into my face. I read it in his eyes – disbelief. Some argument, some quick-witted response was needed. I had always had a sharp tongue, able to defend myself verbally on every occasion. On this day I could think of nothing to say. Already he was turning his attention to old Mrs Huckle who was sitting in the only chair the room possessed.

Dimly, through tears of despair, I saw the visitor touch the old woman's shoulder as she rocked rhythmically to and fro. Then gingerly, he reached out with two fingers to raise Mrs Huckle's right hand by her bony wrist.

'What is this, Mr McCann?' said the visitor.

'Why them, sir, are the leather gloves. You see, each one is actually a leather ball. The hand is thrust into the leather glove and held in place by straps around the wrist. It is for the patient's own protection. This old thing – a pauper lunatic what's been with us these past six years – plucks at her own flesh, making it bleed and doing herself grievous injuries. She pulls out her hair, too, which is why she's nearly bald. And she attacks other patients sometimes. We can't have that.'

All of a sudden – I had never accustomed myself to it – the old woman began to shout obscenities in a high thin voice, spitting into the air as she did so because she had no teeth at all. She wore nothing but a filthy shift that reached half way down her legs, leaving the better part of her wrinkled, bruised flesh exposed. No wonder the visitor released her arm abruptly and moved on.

His gaze fell on Megs who might be thirty or forty or any age in between. The woman herself was in no condition to say. Nothing but skin and bones and dressed in rags, she sat on the floor, her right arm and leg manacled and chained to an iron plate on the wall.

Forgetting his dignity, the visitor squatted on his haunches, the better to see her face. With surprising gentleness, he moved each manacle to study the raw swollen flesh. Her wrist was bleeding. Megs had a distressing habit of pulling against her restraint until she had worn all the skin from her arm. She submitted to the visitor's inspection, showing no interest. Not a flicker of intelligence animated her eyes.

'Take care, she's violent!' said Mr McCann, wiping his face with the ends of his neck-scarf. 'She'd murder somebody if we didn't restrain her.'

'She seems perfectly quiet now.'

'Ah, yes. Now. At this moment, but –'

'Then why not release her until her next violent spell? That at least would give her wounds a chance to heal.'

'Mr Flemynge, it's plain you're one of them men what champions *moral* methods in treating wrongheads, but I'll stake my dinner you ain't seen a madhouse before. You don't know the problems, sir, not by a long chalk. And you don't want to be paying too much attention to them folks as tries to make trouble for the likes of me.

You got to use force with lunatics. And the powders, of course. Why, even Dr Willis himself –'

'Who is Dr Willis? Does he call here?'

McCann looked disgusted. 'No, what would I be wanting with a doctor calling here. I'm an apothecary. My wife and I can do all as is necessary for the patients. There's just ten of them, after all. Dr Willis and his son are only the doctors who attend King George in his madness, that's all. That's who Dr Willis is, and he says the leather glove and other restraints are absolutely vital where you've got lunatics.'

Mr McCann sidled over to a woman patient of sweet expression who had been staring into space for the past hour. 'Let me make you known to Miss Katherine Watson, sir. Miss Watson suffered a terrible blow to the nerves when her gentleman was killed in a riding accident just a week before they were to be married. Mr Flemynge is a magistrate visitor, my dear. Have you something to say to him?'

Katherine Watson curtsied, simpering in a manner that made me fume. The visitor was noticeably impressed by her dainty refinement, clean linen and well-combed hair. I had never imagined I could be so envious of a plain spinster who must be all of thirty-five.

'I do indeed have something to say,' said Miss Watson. 'I am much recovered, which is due entirely to the careful management of Mr and Mrs McCann. And . . . and I hope to be returning to my home shortly,' she finished with a quick pleading look at Mr McCann. 'Of course, I *do* know the date. It is May the twenty-sixth.'

Megs and Mrs Huckle, agitated by this stranger in their midst, had become very noisy. Their screeches were ear-splitting.

'Now, look what you done, Mr Flemynge. Visitors always upset the patients. That's why we don't allow it. Now you've got them all on the twitter and my wife and I will be up half the night attending to them.'

The visitor looked uncertain, confirming McCann's view – and mine – that he had never before been inside a madhouse. 'How many of your patients are paupers paid for by their parishes?' he asked in that chilling voice of his.

'Nine, sir, at nine shillings the week. Two private patients what has their own bedchambers. Miss Watson's family *pays* for her room, but I lets Miss Burns-Roberts have a room of her own out of my compassion. Not that she appreciates my generosity.'

The visitor turned towards me once more, but addressed himself to Mr McCann. 'Miss Burns-Roberts whose aunt and uncle placed her here on January the twenty-second?'

'Yes, sir. And she was in a pitiful state, I can tell you. Howled the place down for days.'

'Wouldn't you have screamed, sir?' I asked. 'Wouldn't you have howled – to use this man's vulgar expression – if you suddenly found yourself locked up in a madhouse? I had been drugged . . . '

The visitor, who had been listening politely to me, now jerked his head towards McCann. The apothecary gave a world-weary shrug. 'What can I tell you, Mr Flemynge? They all say that. I ask you. Why should I do such a thing as to saddle myself with a perfectly sane woman? It would be more trouble than it was worth.'

The visitor rubbed his chin thoughtfully, avoiding my eyes as he moved towards the door. I was defeated. In my heart I had never expected to succeed. The flame of hope that had flared so briefly had been snuffed out by this stranger's coldness, but I murmured accusingly: 'Why have you failed me?'

The visitor might not have heard me. He nodded gravely. 'Good day to you, Miss Burns-Roberts. I wish you a speedy recovery.'

Irritably, Mr McCann wiped his hand on his breeches before turning the doorknob. He was already out of the door and the visitor was halfway through it before helpless fury gave me the strength to cry out: 'Don't you know what they'll do to me for speaking to you?'

He was gone; I sank to the floor and wept bitterly until Mrs Porter knelt down beside me, smirking. Mrs Porter was a plump girl of no more than fifteen who had probably never been married. She spoke continually of her husband, however, and other events that I sincerely hoped could not have occurred.

'I think that man was a magistrate,' said Mrs Porter cheerfully. 'Never seen a magistrate before. Leastways, not that I can remember. You made Mr McCann very angry, dearie. Are you going to fight them when they come for you? That'd be a rare sight, I declare.'

'I'm so afraid,' I whispered.

'And so you should be,' said Mrs Porter and stood up to wander away.

I slid across the floor into a corner and drew up my knees to make myself as small as possible. There was no way of knowing how much time I had left.

Miss Watson had not moved since the visitor left. She just stared into space and let her tears fall upon her gown. Her look of despair was so affecting that I felt a surge of pity, although she had hurt me deeply.

Katherine Watson, daughter of a Suffolk squire, had been delivered to this place at dead of night less than a month ago. She was a private patient and had been taken directly to the cell – it could not be called a bedchamber – next to mine where she had cried heartbrokenly all night.

The next morning, after we had eaten our breakfast of bread and milk, all of us except Megs had been allowed into the female courtyard, a small muddy patch of earth which received no sunlight during the morning. Miss Watson was obviously a sensible woman of good family, so it was natural that she and I should be drawn together. I did not mention my own misfortune, but listened sympathetically for hours as the grieving woman poured out her sad tale – so many years betrothed, but unable to marry because he was a younger son. And then a tragic end to their hopes. Miss Watson's happiness was destroyed, she wished only for death and had tried to take her own life. What was there left for her? A life of drudgery at home, constantly at her mother's beck and call, or sent to help her married sisters when they needed an extra pair of hands.

I, who had come through my own period of terror and hopeless despair, could feel the strongest pity for Miss Watson, especially later in the day when the McCanns began tormenting her. The poor spinster was terrified of them, accustomed as she was to the more subtle forms of bullying employed by her mother.

The next morning Katherine Watson did not put in an appearance at breakfast and I was very worried. However, Mrs Porter, who seemed to know an amazing amount about what went on in the house, told me that in future Miss Watson would be taking all her meals with the McCanns. The new patient was missing all that day, but the next morning we came face to face in the courtyard. It was immediately obvious that Miss Watson was greatly changed. She was calmer, eager to please the McCanns, to sit when told to sit, stand when told to stand, and to control her tendency to tears at least in the presence of her keepers. She had also plainly been told never to speak another word to me.

My only source of intelligent company was now denied me and I felt very bitter about it. It showed a want of character to give in to the McCanns so readily. I knew their ways; I too had suffered. But they could be resisted if one were sufficiently determined. All it required was a little spirit. Then again, it was partly my excessive spirit which had condemned me to this dreadful place. Over the years, I had taught my aunt and uncle to despise me. No wonder they had not hesitated to destroy me when their need for my money arose.

My father, a successful City merchant, died of typhoid fever one terrible day in June, 1806, and my mother survived him by only eight days, leaving me a fourteen-year-old orphan with no living relatives except Uncle Marcus and his childless wife, Aunt Martita. I had lost both the parents I loved dearly and could not even bring myself to be civil to my new guardians.

I, who had been allowed considerable latitude in my own home, spent the next six and a half years in dedicated rebellion. I can't account for my behaviour except to say that it gave me perverse satisfaction to see my aunt quite worn down with the struggle to make me behave respectably.

When I was eighteen, Uncle Marcus found a suitor for me. A well-looking young man of modest fortune came to call one morning. By the time he took my hand to say goodbye fifteen minutes later, I had made sure that he wouldn't want to repeat the experience. Others followed, but my behaviour was always so outrageous that the courtships could not prosper. Before I was twenty, Uncle Marcus had given up the task of choosing a husband for me, and I was so notorious in the neighbourhood for my bad manners that it was unlikely any man would have the courage or the desire to approach me.

Last autumn, at around midnight, I crowned my follies by climbing out of my bedroom window to a nearby tree and escaping into the city streets with no other company than my maid. We walked hand in hand down noisy streets, jeered by roving gangs of apprentice boys. My maid took me to a low inn where we both ordered gin with great bravado, and the maid paid a halfpenny because I had no money at all.

That was the night I met Thaddeus Dawnay. Dear Tad who never called me anything but Bright Star, who laughed a great deal and moved with animal grace, a handsome man with the bluest eyes I have ever seen. Tad bought me a lemonade that night and laughed at my escapade, but he told me I was a naughty puss and insisted on walking me back to my home where he lifted me up into the tree so that I could climb into my room the way I had climbed out of it. Just as well, too, because I discovered that what had been quite easy in the downward direction would have been impossible the other way round without assistance.

Tad and I met this way on four successive nights without mishap. On the fifth, my guardians were waiting for me, and my uncle thrashed me.

Tad came to call the next day and regularly after that. Occasionally, we were given three or four minutes alone together, no more. After a week or two, Tad asked my uncle for my hand in marriage, and I pleaded that since Tad was so much older, I would obey him and make him a good wife. But my uncle had been making enquiries. Tad, a sea captain in former days, now lived on his wits; he was not acceptable. Tad promised me he would never give up hope, and then he stopped calling at the house.

Two weeks later, I was on my way to a convent in Hertfordshire, seated in the coach between my aunt and uncle so that I couldn't escape. Mother Theresa, they told me, would teach me discipline. And Mother Theresa had certainly tried. After six weeks, I, by now something of an expert on the subject of bedroom escapes, left my room late one night. I have a poor sense of direction, but started walking east towards Epping Forest and the High Beech inn where Tad made his home when he was not in London.

It was a cold, tired and hungry girl who finally collapsed in the parlour of the Royal Oak two days later. Tad was not as welcoming as I had hoped. In fact, he scolded me for my wild ways and insisted that for propriety's sake I must share a bedchamber with the innkeeper's wife. Two days later, Uncle Marcus arrived. I never discovered the identity of the informer, although I strongly suspect the innkeeper's wife. We had taken an instant dislike to one another.

The door of the women's day room opened again. Mrs McCann, such a fat contrast to her husband's wiry body, stalked into the room and McCann followed, half-hidden by her bulk. Some deep-seated terror roused Mrs Huckle from her stupor. Throwing up her hands in their grotesque gloves, she flung herself to the ground in a spasm, right in the path of husband and wife. Mrs McCann kicked her aside like a fallen branch, her eyes never leaving mine. In her hands she carried a garment of stiff white duck with long sleeves.

I have a horror of the strait-waistcoat. The dreadful thing had invaded my dreams ever since I had first seen it being worn by Megs. Even leglocks seemed preferable.

In spite of all my good intentions, I leapt up and screamed that I would not be taken, I would fight them with all my strength. The struggle was an unequal one and lasted for only a minute or two, because the McCanns were practised in the business of forcing the inmates to do their bidding. They soon had my arms in the long sleeves, pulling the strings tightly behind me until I was compelled to clutch my own body in a hideous embrace.

They marched me to my cell and forced me to stand while Mrs McCann pulled my hair upwards so that Mr McCann could bleed me from the back of the neck. By the time he announced that he had taken forty ounces, I was too weak to stand unaided.

I passed the rest of the day in torment, trussed up and lying helplessly on my bed. Many hours later, Mrs McCann returned to remove the strait-waistcoat and massage the circulation back into my arms before giving me a bowl of bread and milk.

Some time later they came again, the husband and wife who had taken on the dimensions of demons from hell. I sat up in bed and tried to control my terror as Mr McCann opened a small paper packet and emptied a white powder into half a cup of water. I knew better than to resist. On one occasion, the McCanns had knocked out four of Megs' teeth in an attempt to force her to swallow such a powder.

Mr McCann favoured digitalis to induce vomiting. It was a dangerous drug and had to be administered with care, as he made a point of telling me. So violent was my reaction to it that by the afternoon I felt half dead and lay on my bed, too weak to move. My condition worried the McCanns. They stood by my bedside, and when Mr McCann murmured that my pulse had dropped to forty, his wife said that he had better take care. The treatment was intended to teach me a lesson, not to kill me.

Time slid past in a confusion of waking and sleeping where all dreams were painful and reality was even worse. I was given nothing but bread and milk for three days – or was it four? – and had passed into that state of wretchedness where very little that went on around me could affect my mood.

It was, therefore, rather startling to be awakened from a deep sleep by Mrs McCann who was smiling warmly. 'Up you get, my dear. Here, let me sponge your face with a little warm water. Does that make you feel better? I've washed your dress, do you see? It's still a trifle damp because Bessie had to iron it in a hurry. Slip it on while you sit there. I do believe you are completely recovered! I can see it in your eyes. McCann knows his business, I'll say that for him.'

'This . . . isn't my gown,' I murmured faintly, struggling to come to terms with this new Mrs McCann.

'Of course, it is, my dear. Come now. You must stand up so that I can pull the drawstrings tight.'

I stood up weakly and looked down at the plain white

muslin gown I had never seen before, while Mrs McCann fussed about the drawstrings. She pulled the one threaded through the neckline until I was decently covered and then the one under the bust until the puff-sleeved gown took on a fashionable shape and looked as if it might have been made for me, although it was far too short.

Too confused and ill to argue, I allowed myself to be propelled into the McCanns' small neat parlour – and reeled with the shock of leaving a monochrome world. It was like awakening from the dead. Was there ever a more potent perfume than that of beeswax applied with enthusiasm to dark wood? Its scent conjured visions of home and comfort and security. The McCanns' carpet square was small and old with a pattern that was mostly faded red, but its short tufts caressed the soles of my feet. A yellow milk jug, filled to capacity with wild hyacinths and campion, was a feast for the eyes, and everywhere polished brass gleamed in the sunlight that beamed through the small window.

I had been starved of sensation for so long that now gorging on such beauty left me feeling queasy. I reached for a chairback which proved to be further away than I had judged. I swayed; a comforting hand on my elbow steadied me, and I looked up gratefully into the impenetrable eyes of the magistrate visitor.

'You see, Mr Flemynge?' said Mr McCann with forced heartiness. 'The young lady is in a whole condition as I promised. I have not used violence towards her. As if I would do such a thing!'

'She looks ill.'

'Oh, I had to dose her, sir, as is standard treatment at any establishment. Cupping and the evacuants. I've kept my word, as you should have known I would, for I don't run a cruel home here.' McCann looked regretfully at the scatter of papers on his desk. 'Maybe a few irregularities in the record-keeping. That's as happens to all manner of people.'

'I doubt it.'

'I swear to you . . . A few lapses in the paperwork. I'm no black letter man, never take up a pen if I can help it. That's all there is to it.'

'I shall have my eye on you, McCann.'

'I'm letting the girl go, ain't I? Let that be an end to it. You can't want to close me down. This is my livelihood. How would we eat, the missus and I?' He pointed a finger at me. 'You'll be sorry you've taken on that object. Mark my words. A very independent madam. A trouble-maker. I wish you joy of her.'

'Come, ma'am,' said the visitor coolly. 'Let us be gone from this place. We have some distance to travel.'

With gentle pressure on my arm, he led me towards the door.

# Chapter Two

As we reached the door, a sniff, a tiny half-stifled sob from a high-backed chair by the fireplace told me that Katherine Watson was in the room. Katherine, red-eyed, peeped round the wing of the settle and we stared at one another for several seconds.

'I'll not forget you, Miss Watson,' I said, and was surprised by the weak croaking sound that came from my own throat.

The visitor guided me on to the gravel drive which crunched crisply underfoot. Cinderella's coach! A footman in red and gold livery stood, blank-faced, holding the door of the wine-red travelling chaise. The coachman, immensely superior, sat on his box while matched greys snuffled as they pawed the ground. The footman had apparently made good use of his time while he waited. Every speck of dust and mud had been wiped from the coach. The wheels were so clean that the chaise might have flown here instead of travelling along England's terrible roads.

I put a foot on the footplate, intending to enter the coach, but my weakened muscles wouldn't obey me.

'Mind your head,' said the visitor and lifted me into the coach.

I fell gratefully, if not gracefully, into the far corner, murmuring: 'Blue velvet,' and began to stroke the seat, rubbing the pile first one way and then the other. I was free! My ordeal was over and I never intended to think about it or Chennings again. I would wipe those bleak days from my memory as thoroughly as the coach wheels had been cleaned. I would think only of the future.

The visitor climbed into the coach, making it rock

wildly. He reached past me to let down the window on my side, then sat down next to me and opened the other. A jerk, the crack of a whip and we were off.

I would not have looked back, having no desire to see the outside of Chennings, but the road curved and I saw it all the same; red brick, barred windows, peeling paint. The old house crouched evilly in the sunlight. At the parlour window Katherine Watson's bleak face stared out at me. A silent witness to my inexplicable good fortune.

The sway of the carriage increased my lingering nausea and the sun was too bright. I sank into the fine upholstery and closed my eyes the better to rejoice in my deliverance. I was soon asleep.

In my dreams I was reunited with my parents as we all travelled in our own chaise to the Old Manor House on the escarpment overlooking Cheltenham. How young my mother seemed and how happy my father was! I saw the young Elinor sitting opposite them, scarcely able to contain her excitement. We were to spend the entire summer at my parents' country home, there to meet old acquaintances and make new friends. No hint of the coming disaster marred my vision, no hint of –

'– and so it was the only solution, you see. I hope you do not object.'

The visitor's voice came to me as if from very far away. I opened my eyes and blinked at him. 'I beg your pardon?'

'I was saying, I was enraged when I discovered that a young woman of some refinement had been shut away by her guardians quite illegally. Your uncle hadn't even gone through the motions of obtaining a correct committal document! And heaven knows, such papers are easy enough to acquire. There are too many doctors who are quite willing to sign away some poor devil's freedom. I made up my mind four days ago to take you away from there. Now that you are free, what will become of you? I refuse to return you to your aunt. Do you have a male relative?'

'No, there is no one.'

'I thought not. Otherwise, your uncle would not have dared to act as he did. Miss Burns-Roberts . . . Elinor, you have no choice but to trust me. I am all that stands between you and destitution.'

'You're very kind . . .' I whispered. True, I had no male relative, but there *was* Tad. If only he hadn't been so disapproving when I last saw him!

'I have every intention of looking after you,' said Flemynge, 'but I am a bachelor, you see. Your position would be most uncomfortable if I were to take you home to Thorsby to live. And I will not allow you to live alone. No, there is but one solution. We must be married. For personal reasons, I have set aside for ever all thoughts of a . . . love match. And, if you will permit me to say so, circumstanced as you are, you are unlikely to receive a better offer. I have a ring and a special licence; you are of age. What else can you do?'

*What else?* Marry Tad, of course. Dear laughing Tad. But how to reach him? He was away so much, out of the country for weeks on end. I might . . . but no, I could not go to that inn again. And I saw no point in confronting my aunt. If Uncle Marcus had been, as I suspected, in serious debt when he died, Aunt Martita must be very poor now.

I made a supreme effort to clear my mind. This was important. The visitor must be told. 'Tad . . . that is . . . I'm trying to think. Tad . . .'

He bent closer. 'What's that you say? Today? Yes, I promise you. I think we should be married today, within the hour. I am a tolerably wealthy man, you know. You will find yourself very much more comfortable than of late.' He cleared his throat. 'It will, I needly hardly add, be a marriage in name only. I shall make no demands on you.'

No demands! Needless to say, I had not even considered that point. No demands. No consummation. An annulment later? Yes, that would be possible, surely. And then I could marry Tad. The immediate problem was where to sleep tonight. Sound sleep, safe sleep in a soft bed.

'Elinor, are you asleep?'

I opened my eyes, squinting against the sunlight. 'No, sir. Marry you? I don't know. I can't think clearly. I really do not feel at all well. But it doesn't matter. Yes, if you wish. We will be married.'

'But it does matter! You must think about what I am saying to you. Are you content to marry me? Will you be my wife? Try to understand. This is a commitment for life.'

My eyelids dropped and it was too great an effort to lift them. The concerned expression of the magistrate visitor disappeared and I began to float in a half world between waking and sleep. 'Yes,' I heard myself say, as if from the depths of a tunnel. 'I have thought about it. I will marry you, if you wish. But have we far to go? I am so very tired.'

'Not far,' he said gently. 'In the meantime, try to rest.'

I slept after that, heavily and dreamlessly, and awoke to the feel of a hand on mine. Tad! Squeezing the hand in return, I opened my eyes to look into the startled face of my husband-to-be. Already he was withdrawing his hand, moving away.

'We have almost arrived at the home of the Reverend Smithson. I wanted to wake you in good time.' He removed a large white pocket handkerchief from his sleeve, scrubbed both his hands carefully and pushed the handkerchief home again. The coach came to a stop before a rambling vicarage, and the visitor leapt out as soon as the door was opened for him.

Fortunately, I am not a particularly romantic woman, not one of those young girls who spend idle hours in dreaming of grand weddings. My tastes have always veered towards the unconventional in all matters. I had planned to *elope* with Tad, after all.

The service left no impression on me whatsoever. Only when I sat down to sign the register did it occur to me that I was now married to a man whose full name I hadn't known till that moment. 'Fitzroy James Horatio Flemynge' was written boldly on the page. So I must be *Mrs* Fitzroy James Horatio Flemynge. I tried to imagine myself addressing my new husband as 'Fitzroy', or perhaps as 'Fitzroy, my dear'. Impossible! I would call him Flemynge, which was sufficiently intimate for a marriage of expedience.

We were soon on our way again; the vicar had seemed relieved to wave us goodbye. Flemynge removed the cap from his hip-flask. 'This may revive you,' he said, holding out the flask to me. I shook my head vigorously, remembering my last coach journey. Fortunately, I now felt more alert, able to sit up and look about. I must make some conversation, I thought. He will expect it. But what to say?

'One of the worst things about my stay at Chennings was the feeling of being cut off from all sources of information. Are we still at war with France? What of Wellington?'

He gave my questions serious consideration. 'We are still at war with France. I believe the Marquess is conducting his peninsular campaign with all the cunning and ruthlessness required of a military leader. I do not follow world events very carefully, but you may read about the war in the newspapers when we reach Thorsby Hall.'

I smiled at the way he smoothed the cloth over his thigh, brushing away a mark which only he could see. What long fingers he had! And such a dry way of speaking!

'I used to imagine that the French had invaded England and overrun the country,' I said.

'Such terrifying thoughts are apt to prey on the mind of one situated as you were. I'm sure –'

'Oh, but it wasn't a terrifying thought! I would far rather have been raped by the French than spend the rest of my life locked up in Chennings.'

I heard him gasp. 'You don't know what you are saying!'

'I beg your pardon, sir, but all things are comparative. And I would far rather some villainous Frenchman –' His expression caused me to leave the rest of my sentence unspoken.

Prudish and pedantic! I knew his type. Yes, and how to make his life a misery. He would wish he had never heard of Elinor Burns-Roberts by the time I came to have the marriage annulled. This unnatural marriage would not last for long. Already, I was beginning to doubt the wisdom of it. But what alternative was there? I blinked dreamily and, in spite of my best efforts, went to sleep.

The slowing pace of the horses and the change of surface under their hooves brought me awake. 'Are we home? I'm famished. I've had nothing but bread and milk for several days. Is the pleasant house up ahead your home?'

'Most certainly not,' he said. 'That is Essex Grange. Thorsby Hall is considerably larger. We are paying a brief call and it won't take long, I assure you. I ask this favour of you and shall never ask another. Thorsby is just two miles away from here. When we reach home, you shall eat and have a warm bath and then go straight to bed to recover your strength. Just be patient.'

When we reached the front door of Essex Grange, Flemynge's footman handed me down with great care just as the butler of the house opened the door. I heard the butler exclaim; I heard the footman snigger.

'Barlow, announce Mr and Mrs Fitzroy Flemynge,' said my husband.

'No, sir, I couldn't.'

'Do it!' snarled Flemynge, and the butler fled before us.

The house was charming. Tudor, I think. Its modest hall was a trifle overcrowded with furniture from some larger residence; a very fine Indian carpet, a circular table with a top made of numerous different sorts of marble, and paintings everywhere. I could hardly trust the evidence of my eyes. The paintings had to be copies. If not, this middling-sized country home possessed several still lifes of the Dutch school, a Lely, a van Dyck and other treasures I couldn't immediately identify.

Flemynge had me firmly by the elbow and now pushed me forward as the butler announced us. There were four people in the drawing-room – a family, I supposed, consisting of a young man, a young woman and their parents. I was more interested in the chairs that crowded the room, so many that it would be impossible to walk across the floor with ease. They were fine chairs, gilded and upholstered in woven satin, and they were standing on a beautiful Aubusson carpet so large that it had been ruthlessly turned under down each side of the too-small room.

I was just wondering what sort of eccentric family this could possibly be when I realized that the uproar was on my account. So Flemynge had married to disoblige his family!

'This is my new wife,' said my husband in aggressive tones. 'I have this day fetched her from Chennings madhouse. Since you all profess such an interest in Thorsby Hall, I thought you might care to meet the new mistress. Make your curtsey, Elinor.'

Ashamed and hurt at having been used so cruelly, I looked up at him with tear-filled eyes, then turned to the others and gave a deep curtsey.

'I'll see you in hell!' bellowed the old man whom I presumed to be the father of the two young people – and

Flemynge also? 'A wife from the madhouse, you say? She is the perfect mate for you. You are trying to destroy us, but you won't succeed. You can't destroy the Presscotts, and even a lunatic cannot dim the beauty of Thorsby.'

I felt myself going faint, but Flemynge's arm held me rigidly upright. 'I am quite sure you are right,' he said. 'I am also certain that she will conduct herself with greater dignity and decency than the previous occupants of Thorsby. She comes from Chennings, it's true, but she is honest. *She* wouldn't presume to appropriate an estate to which she had no claim. So I think she will make a vastly superior mistress of Thorsby.'

'You damned knave! You bastard! Would you insult my mother?' cried the young man, the handsome son, who bore no resemblance whatsoever to Flemynge.

'Why, no, sir.' Flemynge ignored me as I tugged at his sleeve. 'I didn't say to whom she is superior. It was not a comparison, to be sure. I say, merely, that she will make a superior mistress of Thorsby.'

The old man clutched his chest and flung out his hand to steady himself on a chairback. 'Now see what you have done,' said the plump mother, surely much younger than her husband. 'Get out of this house! Haven't you done enough? In the name of God, go!'

'Yes, let us go,' I said, and Flemynge nodded his assent. All the while, the daughter of the house, a slim girl in her twenties, had remained strangely calm. She wore a pale green gown so skimpily cut that it revealed every bone in her body. Our eyes met and she gave me such a malevolent look that I sucked in my breath in surprise. They all hated me, surely, but the girl's burning eyes were especially upsetting.

'Your servant, Mrs Presscott,' said Flemynge cordially. 'Your servant, Miss Presscott. Since we have not been invited to take tea with you, we had better be on our way. Do call on us at Thorsby. You will be welcome at any time, I assure you.' He turned and led me from the room, walking so swiftly that I was obliged to trot and stumble after him.

We reached the long drive of Thorsby Hall within minutes. During that time, Flemynge had not chosen to speak and I had not the strength to do so. I understood now. I had been fetched from Chennings to play my part in some kind of feud.

My first sight of Thorsby confused me even more. It was a palace. No, I exaggerate. A very fine country house, then, a suitable home for a wealthy and important man. Worth fighting for, I supposed. If I stayed, would Flemynge really expect me to be mistress of all this?

The house was built in the shape of a horseshoe, the main block being three storeys high with a central pediment. Single-storey colonades swept in elegant curves from right and left linking smaller blocks at the ends of the horseshoe. The house was red brick, but stone dressing emphasized the perfect lines of the architect's plan. I was still sitting like a stone, lost in admiration when a liveried servant opened the carriage door to help me out.

The interior of Thorsby was as impressive as the outside: a large hall bisected by a wall of marble pillars and arches. A staircase of noble proportions that would allow a regiment to march up it, at least until they reached the landing where the staircase split and dog-legged back on itself. Yes, the hall was certainly impressive, not simply because of the marble floor nor the glass dome in the roof which bathed this vast space in glowing light. The hall impressed because it was entirely unfurnished.

There were no carpets on the floor nor ornaments of any kind. Pale rectangles on the light blue walls indicated where paintings had once hung. There was neither a chair nor a table in sight, nowhere to put one's letter tray, nowhere to dispose of a visitor's hat and gloves.

And now I understood a good deal more about the feud. Flemynge had the house; the Presscotts had the furniture.

The butler, a youngish man introduced to me as Grimsby, led the way through a substantial mahogany door at the top of the stairs. The room we entered had once been a grand bedroom. Now, a modest bed with dirty muslin hangings sat baldly on the bare boards. Magnificently swagged old yellow curtains hung from the large windows beneath gilded wooden pelmets. There was, as I recall, a dressing-table, a looking glass on a stand, a cane-seated chair, a small gate-legged table and a clothes press with chipped veneer.

I rubbed my forehead wearily. I had been given too much to think about all in one day. I wanted to scream at my husband, but did not dare. Truth to tell, I was afraid of him. Elinor Burns-Roberts, who had never been afraid of a man in her life, found this silent gentleman very frightening indeed.

'I have only recently taken possession of the house,' said Flemynge. 'You may help me to choose some new furnishings. I have some catalogues somewhere.' I couldn't meet his eye, but nodded dully.

The butler bowed himself out as the housekeeper, a maid and a young kitchen girl, who was struggling with an enamel bath, came into the room.

'This is Mrs Hobson, the housekeeper,' said Flemynge, indicating a neat woman in her forties. 'Millichip will be your personal maid.' He then smiled in quite a civilized way at the kitchen maid. 'I don't know your name. Have I seen you before?'

The child opened her mouth to reply but Mrs Hobson spoke for her. 'That is Bates, sir. She is the daughter of one of your tenants. I had to take on some extra people since so many of the staff went with . . . have left. Run along, Bates, and fetch the water for madam's bath. You will be wanting to bathe and change your clothes, Mrs

Flemynge. If Mr Flemynge would care to go downstairs where some refreshments have been laid out . . .?'

Flemynge took the hint. 'I shall return when you are dressed, Elinor.'

I took several deep breaths, summoning the strength to walk over to the nearest of the four tall windows. The room overlooked the garden at the back of the house, now taking the full force of the afternoon sun. I am no connoisseur of gardens, heaven knows. As a child of the smoky City, I found few enough opportunities to visit grand gardens. All the same, I had no doubt that the one laid out so beautifully below me was very fine indeed. Stone balustrades surrounded a broad terrace, a delightful place in which to take one's promenade, although probably too hot on the sunniest days of summer.

Wide steps led invitingly to green lawns which undulated as they sloped gently away into the distance. Nature had been artfully enhanced to please the eye: here a clump of trees, there a few sheep grazing. Over to the right was an old oak tree creating an oasis of shade. I could just make out a wooden seat built right round the trunk. The focal point of the view was the lake at the bottom of the slope, fingers of light bouncing off its broken surface as it curved out of sight.

Just like Chennings, I thought, and smiled to myself. Resting my head against the opened shutters, I tried to concentrate, tried to assess my position. Married to a stranger! Whatever had I done? True, I was free of the madhouse, had a comfortable bed and the prospect of good food for the rest of my life. Thorsby was a magnificent home. To be mistress of all this certainly had its attractions.

But my dreams of controlling my own life and making my own decisions had been destroyed. Flemynge had seen to that. My new husband was no kind-hearted fool to be manipulated at will. He had removed me from Chennings, and even married me, presumably to wreak some sort of vengeance on the family at Essex Grange. For a man to go to such lengths for revenge, suggested a nature of almost unbelievable ruthlessness.

I dreaded the thought of telling him that I wished to have the marriage annulled. If he didn't want to free me, he would find a means of preventing the annulment.

'If madam would come to the bath to allow Millichip to remove her clothing . . .' said Mrs Hobson diffidently. The housekeeper was all starch and flashy efficiency, but the smile pinned to her face did little to conceal her embarrassment.

Millichip was a clumsy woman of enormous size. I guessed that she had never been a maid before. Nervousness made the country girl all thumbs as she tried to unhook the muslin gown at the back.

'I can't seem to do anything correctly, ma'am,' Millichip giggled, an unnerving sound from such a large person.

'Don't be nervous,' I said. 'Let us move in front of the looking glass where I can see what you are doing.'

I walked over to the cheval mirror with Millichip in tow still fussing with the hooks and eyes, and for the first time since January saw myself in a glass. It was the last straw. Of course I had known my feet were bare and my gown was too short and my hair had not been touched by a comb for weeks. But knowing and seeing were two different things. Frantically, I pulled a strand of matted hair, plucked at the ridiculously short gown, rubbed at the smears of dirt on my neck, all the while too shocked to talk or even to make a squeak of despair. Finally, all the stresses of the day combined to breach the dam of my self-control. Then I could not stop speaking, hysterically and at the top of my voice.

'My God! What has happened to me? My beautiful hair! Look, look! Is this how I looked when that villain took me to Essex Grange? Before those people? Gaping and sneering at me . . . a peepshow. How they must have laughed, or no, not laughed. Mistress of Thorsby, he said. The cruellest joke in the world. The brute! The swine! I'll kill him for this! No, I'd rather die. I can't face myself, a ragamuffin, a dreadful, filthy slut. Get me a pair of scissors immediately!'

'Oh, no, madam!' cried Millichip in alarm and Mrs Hobson ran to the door to call Flemynge.

'There you are, you heartless coward!' I cried when he burst into the room. 'Making a fool of me for your own purposes. And I thought you were kind. Evil deceiver, that's what you are. Did it never occur to you that I might have feelings? How dare you drag me into Essex Grange, before civilized people, looking as I do? I'll never forgive you, do you hear me? I'll make you sorry you treated me this way. How many times do I have to say it? *Get me a pair of scissors!*'

'Get out,' said Flemynge to the servants and both women were quick to obey, shutting the door behind them. 'What difference does it make to you how you looked at the Grange? I asked for that one favour. A brief call before you were cleaned up. You don't know those people. You need never see them again. I had my reasons.'

'Yes, to shock them. To hurt them. And me. What kind of man are you?'

'The sort who will not put up with temper tantrums.' Flemynge took me by the shoulders, twirled me round until my back was towards him, took my wrists, crossed my arms in front of me and held my hands at my waist. Then he obliged me to return to the looking glass.

'Look at yourself, my girl. See how disgracefully you are behaving. Have you no self-control whatsoever?'

'I don't want to look at myself,' I said, turning my head away. 'Please don't hold me like this. Please, please. Just get me a pair of scissors.'

'Certainly not. Why? So that you can end your life? Or is it my life you would finish?'

I jerked my head up to look at his image in the glass. 'Oh, you silly man! Have you no sense? I just want to cut my hair. It is the only way to deal with the tangles.'

He dropped my hands abruptly and went to the door. 'Millichip, get your mistress a pair of scissors. Her hair must be cut before it is washed.' He closed the door and turned to look at me, having almost lost control of his temper at last. 'I have been called a great many names during my life, but no one has ever called me silly.'

'No?' I said through gritted teeth. 'But then you haven't been married for very long, have you?' To my annoyance, a ghost of a smile flickered across his face.

He left when Millichip and Mrs Hobson returned. I sat down at the dressing-table, unable to hold back the tears. At one time, my hair had been my greatest vanity. It is titian, thick and naturally curly. Tad used to say it had sunbeams in it.

The cutting was a surprisingly lengthy business, and I was finally left with just four inches all over my head. However, when it had been washed and combed, it did curl rather attractively. I was impressed by Mrs Hobson's skill and said so.

After I had bathed, Millichip fetched a nightgown and a sea-green negligée which she laid out on the bed.

'It's too early to put on night things,' I said. 'I haven't had my dinner.'

'You are to have it in here, madam,' said Mrs Hobson brightly. 'Coddled eggs and a nourishing rice pudding. Won't that be nice? And so ... nourishing. Mr Flemynge felt sure you would want to rest.'

'Yes, I suppose he is right. I wish I didn't feel so weak.' I studied my reflection in the glass. 'This is a very fine negligée? Where did it come from?'

'Why, Mr Flemynge had it made for you, madam,' said Mrs Hobson. 'I've collected a wardrobe of sorts for you as Mr Flemynge said you might not have any clothing with you.' She opened the clothes press to display shawls, undergarments, two morning dresses and an evening gown with an over-tunic.

'My husband arranged all of this for me?' I asked suspiciously.

'Yes, madam. The dressmakers are quite exhausted. I was forced to purchase some items ready-made, of course. How much can two women sew in just four days?'

At long last, the paraphernalia of the bath was cleared away, together with my old clothes. The little gate-legged table was set for one, and Flemynge entered at the same time as a footman carrying the dinner tray.

'A great improvement,' he said calmly, as if there had been no quarrel. He had removed his coat and cravat, and looked far less forbidding.

I could not meet his eye, feeling all the self-consciousness of a woman who knows that she has been going everywhere smelling like a pigsty. I was clean now, but, perversely, never felt dirtier. Besides, I had made a scene, screamed like a fishwife. He had seen me at my very worst while never losing his own iron control. To cover my chagrin, I held out one arm and flicked the deep lace at the negligée's cuff.

'This wrapper is really very beautiful.' Could he hear the tremor in my voice? 'Do you think it suits me?' I turned round slowly so that he might admire it. 'I understand you had it made for me.'

'Yes, I did. I knew McCann would have sold your clothes. That is the type of man he is. So I ordered a few things to be made as soon as I decided that I must take you away from Chennings. Wait! What has happened to the back of your neck? Did they cut you with the scissors?'

'No, that is where McCann bled me.'

'Good Lord, I had forgotten!' He turned, opened the door and went out on to the landing. 'You down there! Send up a bottle of burgundy and two glasses!'

I sat down to eat the eggs before they became unpalatably cold, but looked up with amusement when he returned. 'Doesn't the bell work?'

'Yes, but not as quickly as my method. How many ounces did he take from you? Do you know?'

'He said forty.' I frowned. 'And . . . and I must beg of you, never to hold me that way again. I can't bear it.'

'What way?' he asked blankly, and I stood up to demonstrate, crossing my arms around my body.

'Like the strait-waistcoat.' I felt hot tears prick my eyes yet again and turned away. 'I . . . just can't bear it, that's all. Please don't do it again.'

'Did McCann put a strait-waistcoat on you?'

I nodded. 'Immediately after you left.'

'He will pay for the way he treated you. It was quite improper.'

I reached for the rice pudding. 'Why did he allow you to take me away? You must have threatened him. Was it because I was being held illegally?'

'The law says that a medical certificate confirming insanity is required before non-paupers like yourself can be confined. There was no proper certificate. In the circumstances, McCann dared not refuse to let you go. His record-keeping in other respects is poor. He is, in short, a rogue. I will deal with him in the future.'

'What good are laws if they can be so easily flouted?'

'Why, none! No certificate at all is required on behalf of paupers. They can be locked away for ever. The only reason that they are released from time to time is that the parish doesn't want to continue to pay for their keep. You, on the other hand, might have been left to rot in that place.'

'Don't say that. I can't bear to think about it.'

'I, myself, ignored the law, I'm afraid. I should have been accompanied by a doctor on my first visit, but I didn't know of one I could trust. Colonel Sotherby, the Chairman of the Bench, was responsible for my becoming a magistrate, and since inspecting madhouses is one of the more time-consuming and unpleasant duties of members of the bench I, as the newest member, was given the task.'

There was a soft knock on the door and Flemynge walked over to open it. After a brief whispered conversation, he returned to the table carrying a tray on which stood a bottle of burgundy, a glass and a tin mug. He filled the glass and held it out to me.

'Drink it all. It will restore your blood.' He poured a generous measure into the cup. 'Your health! I must buy some glasses one of these days.'

'Is this house entirely empty?'

'Scarcely a stick. No furniture in the dining-room though it's as big as a barn, more for state occasions than every-day eating. The morning-room will be easier to heat on a cold day, I'm sure, and much easier to furnish. The drawing-room, salon, ante-rooms, library, what-have-yous, all empty. The kitchen staff have had to buy what they need at short notice. The estate requires a staff of forty, I'm told. I said fifteen would have to do, but I see Mrs Hobson is already adding to her empire.'

A footman knocked and entered with a second bottle of wine. I couldn't imagine what had become of the contents of the first bottle, but when I stood up I knew at once that I must have helped to empty it.

Flemynge filled glass and cup again; this time we drank in silence. Since there was only one chair, he sat on the side of the bed, his long legs easily reaching the floor, although the bed was a high one.

This is my wedding day, I thought, acutely aware of Flemynge as a man. I could actually see hair on his chest, an intimate and faintly embarrassing glimpse of my lawful husband. And here I sat, bold as you please, in my nightgown and negligée just as if it were the most natural thing in the world. Yet I didn't know this man at all. I should be here with Tad, I thought, with the man I love. That would seem right and proper.

Making a great effort to appear unconcerned, I studied my husband carefully. He was puzzling. Pompous and prudish one minute, the next drinking wine from a tin mug as if he didn't care about possessions or status at all. Seeing him seated at his ease on the bed, it was hard to remember how coarsely he had behaved at Essex Grange.

I finished my wine; he waved the bottle casually and I walked rather unsteadily towards him with my glass held out before me.

'I don't expect you to drink so freely every day,' he said with mock severity.

I gave him a slightly coquettish look, not at all sure what manner to adopt towards him. The wine had loosened the tension in my bones, deadened the wariness that had kept me safe and mentally sound over the recent months. I should be outraged by this man's behaviour and his callous manipulation. He had acted disgracefully and any person with an ounce of pride would be furious. *I* should be furious, but a woman situated as I was could not afford such luxuries as outrage. Perhaps he had his reasons for what he had done. I decided to forgive him, and if that was not possible, at least I could push the incident to the back of my mind and start afresh. My strategy must be to play the perfect little wife until I was ready to leave.

Walking round to the other side of the bed, I sat down. 'Who were those people we visited this afternoon?'

'The Presscotts. Hildebrand Presscott, his wife, Amanda, his charming son, Aubrey, and his daughter, Lucinda. They used to live here. The old man was my mother's husband. Mama had an affair with Presscott's secretary and ran away with him when she discovered she was pregnant. She and Presscott were divorced shortly before I was born. No matter. The house is entailed to the first born, male or female, illegitimate or not, and comes to me from my mother. She inherited it from her grandmother. I was always the heir and old Presscott knew it. The Presscott family had no right to live here all those years while Mama and I lived in rented rooms.'

I blinked, taking in not only Flemynge's illegitimacy but the matter-of-fact way in which he told me. Years of hiding the pain had given him a hard shell. 'Why didn't your mother demand her house, especially after the divorce? But then doesn't a woman's property become her husband's when they marry?'

'Usually. It depends on the titles, how the thing was set up. This house was always my mother's as was the revenue from the estate, but she didn't understand. Women don't take a great interest in business matters when they are young and have male relatives to think for them. My grandfather could have told her she was entitled to five thousand pounds a year. Instead, he made her an allowance of two hundred pounds a year and never spoke to her again, not even when she lay on her deathbed. When Grandfather died a month ago, my mother's brother, my Uncle Alfred Flemynge, contacted me and suggested that I seek redress through the law, which I did.'

'But your father —'

'My father had the good sense to overturn his carriage in a drunken stupor before I was born,' he said bitterly. 'He was, by all accounts, a hell-for-leather man with more hair than wit.'

'I see. So distressing for you.' What else could I say? 'This house must have had many treasures in it, collected over the years. Why did you let them take everything?'

'No inventory could be found, no record of what belonged to the estate. I was suspicious, of course, but determined to remove the Presscotts from the premises as quickly as possible. I wanted Thorsby, and now I have it. I might also have pursued them through the courts for thirty years' income from the estate, but as you see, I am not vindictive.'

'No, of course you're not,' I said drily. He had been out-manouevred over the furniture and it rankled with him. Let him try to hide his annoyance; I wasn't fooled.

Abruptly, he turned away and walked over to the bell-pull. 'I was forgetting. You must be very tired. Go to bed and sleep well. I must go to York on business and –'

He was at the door before I recovered from my surprise. 'Flemynge!'

'Well?'

'I am grateful to you for taking me away from Chennings. And . . . and I suppose that is all I wanted to say.'

I had embarrassed him. 'My only concern is your good health. Good night, Elinor.'

# Chapter Three

I awoke with the birds next morning. Feeling restless and hungry, I dressed quickly and slipped as quietly as possible down the broad marble staircase, taking a good look round as I went. The beginnings of a beautiful summer day flooded the bare hall with light, enhancing the sense of emptiness, revealing how the heart had been torn out of the place. Those who loved this house had moved away. Flemynge desired Thorsby, but he had no love for it, I thought, as I opened a pair of doors behind the main staircase.

The salon – what other room would be so richly decorated, drawing the eye upwards to an extravagance of geometrical patterns in gilt and azure? This grand room had lost its power. Now the eye was drawn irresistibly to what was missing. The carpet was gone, leaving behind the dull wood block floor surrounded by a border that had been richly polished over the years. The paintings were gone and the brocaded walls were marked with their rectangular ghosts. With a shudder, I closed the doors quickly and moved on. The drawing-room, the main dining-room and the ballroom all stood forlorn, distinguished one from the other only by what they lacked.

After a walk along one colonnaded promenade, I reached the library which made up a square at the end of one part of the horseshoe. Shelves, surprisingly still lined with books, clothed the walls wherever there was space. A dainty curving staircase led to a narrow gallery running round three sides of the room which put more books within easy reach.

However, when I had climbed the stairs, faded

Morocco bindings and neatly blocked gold lettering on the spines showed me nothing more enticing than Pliny; some dry accounts of skulduggery in former times; bound volumes of the *Gentleman's Magazine*; and treatises on natural history. I assumed that the books had proved too much trouble to steal. Or perhaps the Presscotts were not a scholarly family.

I was rather puzzled by some small stacks each of four or five books – obviously taken from the shelves – placed side by side along one wall. Were these to be discarded, sent to the Presscotts as their own, or perhaps merely placed there to weigh down some lifting floorboards? Too hungry to give the matter serious thought, I closed the door and headed back to the main building to explore the other side of the house.

Eventually, and rather to my surprise, I found a set of three plain rooms of modest size; no gilding or plasterwork here. This suite would be where the Presscott family had lived from day to day. Unlike the rest of the house, these rooms needed decorating. Already, ideas were forming in my mind.

The other colonnade – partially open to the elements like its twin – led to the domestic offices. All our food would have to be carried from the kitchen along this route to the small dining-room, which would guarantee cold meals. Efficiency and comfort obviously had not weighed heavily with the architect.

The kitchen was large, old-fashioned and only scantily furnished. I marvelled at the pettiness of the out-going family; they must have taken every pot, pan and dishcloth. If I had been Flemynge's wife at the time of the Presscott's departure, I would have seen to it that they had left everything behind for which they couldn't prove ownership.

The housekeeper's room and other offices mirrored the library; there was a very creditable servants' hall which was properly furnished. I found half a dozen members of staff – the men in their shirtsleeves – seated at a long table eating hearty breakfasts and drinking quantities of ale. Neither Mrs Hobson nor Grimbsy was present, but I saw the Bates girl and smiled at her. The servants were stunned to silence, setting down their tankards the better to concentrate on staring rudely.

'I know it is early,' I said, speaking to them all, 'but I have been asleep for a long time and I am now very hungry. I would like my breakfast, please. Roast beef and eggs served as soon as possible. I suppose I will have to eat it in my room.'

'It's just gone half past six, madam!' said one young man. 'Chef's not up yet.'

They were still staring at me in a disconcerting manner, when Mrs Hobson hurried into the room. 'Mrs Flemynge! Whatever is the matter?'

'I've slept long enough and I am hungry. I've been exploring the house and would now like to have a substantial breakfast. I won't be up so early tomorrow morning, I can assure you. We will soon get into some sort of routine, Mrs Hobson. But this morning I would like to eat right away.'

'Would half an hour be all right, Mrs Flemynge? I can see that your breakfast is served at seven o'clock, if that is agreeable.'

'Seven o'clock will be quite all right. Meanwhile I will take a walk in the grounds. Please send someone for me when my meal is ready.'

I left them all still staring. As soon as I was out of sight, I checked my dress, but found that there were no hooks left embarrassingly undone. One would have thought by the servants' reaction that I was a creature from another planet.

When I had looked into the spider-inhabited gazebo and walked all the way down the hill, the pleasure of being abroad in the early morning began to pall, so I was pleased when a footman, now correctly dressed in his red and gold livery, came trotting across the lawn to fetch me.

Mrs Hobson was waiting in my room, considerably more composed than she had been earlier. 'Here we are, Mrs Flemynge, a substantial breakfast, as you requested. I hope it is still hot. I'm sorry that there is nowhere else for you to eat . . . Everything is so –'

'It is really not important, but my husband and I must certainly buy some furniture as soon as possible. We can hardly continue in our present style. By the way, what time does Mr Flemynge normally rise?'

'Well, *normally* he rises at half past eight, but I believe his valet, Caxton, woke him at five o'clock this morning.'

'Five o'clock? But then where is he? Has he eaten his breakfast?'

Mrs Hobson twisted her hands together nervously. 'He has gone away.'

I laid down my cutlery and looked closely at the housekeeper's unhappy face. The woman's eyes slid away. 'Where has he gone?'

'To York, ma'am. Caxton went with him.'

I bit my lip in vexation. He had said something about York, but I hadn't been listening too closely. 'When do you expect him back?'

'Mrs Flemynge, he didn't tell us when to expect him. He has only lived in this house for two weeks. We don't know his habits. He doesn't say very much and –'

'Did he leave a message for me?'

'Just to say that he was going to York, but he left instructions that . . . that is . . . you are to have whatever you wish.'

'Very well. I want the carriage sent round within half an hour. How far away is High Beech?'

'Madam, you can't take the carriage out! I mean you mustn't. It would be more than my job is worth.'

'Really? I wonder why. Don't tell me, let me guess. The horses are all lame.'

'Of course not!'

'Very well then, the coachmen are all lame. Come now. What is the reason that I can't order my husband's coachman to take me out when I am to have whatever I wish?'

Mrs Hobson, faced with the necessity of speaking plainly, was deeply distressed. Fortunately for her, a hidden door in the wall burst open at that moment and Millichip blundered in.

'Oh, madam, I'm ever so sorry. I didn't hear you get up. Surely, it is very early! I hadn't expected you to be such an early riser.'

I stared at the little door in some surprise, not having noticed it the day before. It was made to fit flush with the wall and was decorated in exactly the same way, with a chair-rail and white paint below, yellow brocade above. When it was closed, it was virtually undetectable. Even Mr McCann had not had such a handy means of spying on his sleeping inmates.

'You were told your duties, young lady,' said Mrs Hobson sternly. 'You must contrive in future not to sleep so heavily.'

'It doesn't matter,' I said. 'I doubt very much if I'll ever rise so early again. Go downstairs and have your breakfast, Millichip. I wish to go for a long walk into and around the nearest village in about an hour.'

'Oh no, madam!' cried the maid.

'Please do not say "oh no, madam" to me,' I said. 'I don't like it. Practise saying "oh yes, madam" and we shall get on a great deal better. I am going for a walk later this morning and I want you to accompany me. If you do not, then you are dismissed and I will walk alone.'

'Oh no, ma–' began Millichip and clapped a hand over her mouth as she looked at Mrs Hobson.

'Suppose you go downstairs and have your breakfast as madam suggested,' said Mrs Hobson. 'I will join you directly.'

When the big mahogany door had closed behind the maid, I turned to Mrs Hobson. 'Now let us stop talking in circles. Has my husband issued instructions that I am not to leave the grounds until he returns?'

'Those were his orders, I'm afraid.'

'Is he always so autocratic? But I was forgetting; you don't know his habits. What a pity that he didn't tell me about it yesterday. The man is as slippery as an eel. We don't know how long he will be gone, nor how to reach him if there should be an emergency. It might be months. But no, not even Flemynge would leave me situated as I am for more than a few days.'

By this time I was in no doubt that the staff believed me to be dangerously mad. Flemynge had unwittingly given them the wrong impression about me, and as a result I had exchanged one prison for another. Of course, walking in the extensive grounds would be very pleasant after months of being so closely confined, and the food was excellent. Nevertheless, I was not really so much better off here than at Chennings. I was still separated from Tad and still unable to contact him, because I had no doubt that Mrs Hobson and the others would prevent me from sending a letter to anyone. This had to remain a supposition; my pride prevented me from asking Mrs Hobson about sending letters. Flemynge had caused me enough embarrassment for one day.

'What am I to do all day when the house is empty and I must not leave it?'

'Mr Stornaway might be able to advise you,' said Mrs Hobson. 'He is the land steward and could arrange for you to make some purchases. I know Mr Flemynge left definite instructions with him about your pin money.'

'Where shall I meet this man? I can hardly entertain him here in my bedchamber.'

'Yes, madam, it is awkward. However, Mr Stornaway has a suite of offices leading off the library. That is where he can usually be found when he isn't out visiting the tenants or the farms.'

The door leading from the library to the land agent's offices was also cunningly hidden. I had to spend some time searching and finally found it, disguised with bookshelves, behind the circular staircase. There was a narrow passageway beyond the secret opening, with a broad, cream-painted door on the right.

'Come in,' said a deep voice in answer to my knock. A sportingly dressed middle-aged man looked up with a frown as I walked into the room. 'Well?'

'Mr Stornaway? I am Mrs Flemynge.'

He scrambled to his feet, straightening his cravat. 'I beg your pardon, madam. I didn't expect to see you here in my office. Welcome to Thorsby.'

Mr Stornaway's words were polite enough, but he delivered them without a smile, without warmth. He doesn't like me, I thought, and the feeling is mutual. He was a portly man in his fifties with a fringe of white hair and extraordinary black eyebrows which grew straight out from his forehead. His complexion was coarse and red, and his small mouth suggested a mean disposition.

'I've come to discuss a number of things with you,' I said coolly. 'My allowance, for one thing, and we must order some furniture as soon as possible. We cannot go on as we are.'

'If Mr Flemynge had not gone away so soon after your arrival –'

'And if you had not let the Presscotts rob this house of its furniture, we wouldn't be in this pickle, would we?' I interrupted, and immediately regretted it. It was unwise to make an enemy of this man.

His face had gone a shade redder. 'There was no proof of ownership, Mrs Flemynge.'

'How long have you been land steward on this estate?'

'For ten years, but I don't see what –'

'Yet you never drew up an inventory. Strange.

However . . .' He opened his mouth to speak and I rushed ahead. ' . . . I have come here to talk of other things. I'm sure you have your reasons for allowing so much valuable property to be carted away. Was that quite within the law, I wonder?'

'I will discuss this matter with Mr Flemynge, madam, not with you! Your husband made no complaint at the time. The Presscotts lived here long before I came to the district. I had no reason to suspect them of behaving incorrectly. *They* have always been regarded in this neighbourhood as decent people.' His subtle emphasis on the word 'they' angered me, but reminded me that I was the unknown intruder. Besides, I remembered that I was furious with Flemynge for a number of reasons. He would have to fight his own battles.

'How much will I be given each quarter as pin money?'

Mr Stornaway didn't answer immediately. He was breathing rapidly and appeared to be considering whether or not he wished to continue the conversation at all. I gave him what I hoped was a rueful, engaging smile. 'Let us not quarrel, Mr Stornaway. I was at fault. I know I must not interfere in the affairs of men.'

Slightly mollified, he sat down again. 'Mr Flemynge realized that you would need to purchase many, many things, since you arrived with nothing of your own. I am authorized to pay for anything you wish to buy – clothing, incidentals and even some furnishings for the family rooms.'

'But the ridiculous thing is,' I said with a laugh, 'the servants believe I have been forbidden to leave the grounds. This is an oversight on the part of my husband. Or perhaps he thought I might come to grief on my own. If you would be willing to give up one full day to take me to the nearest large town, I could buy all the necessities. I'm sure Mr Flemynge would feel I was perfectly safe with you, Mr Stornaway.'

Stornaway looked aghast. 'I'm not prepared to take the responsibility, Mrs Flemynge. When your husband returns from his travels, he can take you about if he thinks it wise. Until then, you may write out a list of whatever you require and my wife will undertake to make all the purchases. We plan to travel up to London tomorrow on personal business. As for the funiture, I have some catalogues here –'

'What responsiblity? Why should Mr Flemynge think it *unwise* to take me anywhere?'

'Now madam, pray don't upset yourself. Your nerves are not yet what they should be. I was told of your distress upon seeing yourself in the looking glass –'

'Do you spend much of your time gossiping with the servants, Mr Stornaway?' I asked sarcastically. But what was the point of getting angry? As a result of the ill-judged visit to Essex Grange, the entire neighbourhood would be agog with the news that a lunatic was mistress of Thorsby. I was a fool not to have guessed what they must be thinking, but Flemynge was responsible for this. He should have foreseen the embarrassment to myself that would be the consequence of his actions.

I stood and lifted my chin proudly. 'I am a good deal saner than you think, Mr Stornaway.'

Stornaway wore a twisted smile as he, too, stood up. 'There may be some justice in your claim, madam. However, to be fair, you perhaps do not appreciate the extent of your illness. Your husband must be the proper judge of your condition. Remember, you belong to him now. If you will make out your list, my wife or one of my staff will bring back to you everything you need to make you perfectly comfortable.'

Resigned for the moment to the present state of affairs, I begged some paper and a pencil from him, took up the furnishing catalogues and went to my chamber. For over an hour I wrote hurriedly, putting down everything I could conceivably need, from a nail-file to a dining-table and eight chairs. When I had finished, I rang for a footman to collect the list and deliver it to the land steward, then I lay down on the bed and closed my eyes.

My situation was galling in the extreme. I could not simply walk out of Thorsby, not yet at least. Tad had behaved very callously towards me when I had followed him to the Royal Oak. I was determined not to risk such a rebuff again. He must be contacted, certainly, and told of my situation. But I would not crawl to him.

In the meantime, falling into despair would solve nothing. I forced myself to relax, to lie perfectly still on the bed, creating mental images of sunlight and green grass, mellow brick and stone walkways, of drifting on a cloud. I must have been extremely tired, because I slept for several hours and awoke knowing exactly what I must do.

I had no money, it was true, but Flemynge had an income of five thousand pounds a year. I would relieve him of some of it. I would send for the dressmaker and the milliner. I would order shoes by the dozen and laces and ribbons and anything else that came to mind. And over the weeks – perhaps months – I would collect some hard cash. Running-away money.

I concentrated hard, remembering my husband's thoughtlessness; anger could be a powerful tonic, stimulating the blood circulation and clearing the mind. But where could he be? And how long would this unbearable loneliness last? Better to have him at home in this great empty house where I could rail at him, than to live in such utter isolation, because there was no getting round it; the only person to whom I could talk as an equal, the only person who knew my circumstances and knew that I was sane, was Flemynge.

Flemynge's departure fortunately coincided with a spell of fine weather. The dressmaker was eager to please, brimming with ideas for summer gowns and capable of executing her most daring designs within forty-eight hours. Whatever pleasure and comfort a woman may derive from new clothes, I had in abundance.

Mrs Stornaway, although incapable of meeting my eye and speaking to me in a natural way, did not fail me in the matter of purchasing necessities. Morever, she brought me several three-volume novels and everything I could want for painting in watercolours, which had always been my favourite pastime.

I read in the privacy of my room, beneath the oak tree and on the terrace. I painted the lake, the house, and myself with the aid of a looking glass. I also tried, but without success, to obey my mother's most often repeated advice: count your blessings.

The books failed to distract me and the paintings were disappointing. By the time Flemynge had been away for seven whole days, I was so irritable that no servant dared speak to me, although they all added to my frustration by spying on me continually.

On the morning of the eighth day, I put on my new lavender muslin gown, dressed my hair with great care, added a broad-brimmed chip-straw bonnet and went out on to the terrace by way of the unfurnished saloon. As I leant against the balustrade wondering how to fill yet another day, I heard the sound of a man's booted feet striding across the saloon and on to the flagstones. So grateful was I that Flemyge had come back, I had to resist the temptation to turn around and fling my arms about his neck.

Instead, I reminded myself how lonely I had been and how annoyed I was with him, and continued to stare out over the lawns. 'It is about time you returned,' I said over my shoulder. 'Do you realize what suffering you have caused me?'

'I beg your pardon?' said a strange voice and I whirled round to stare in embarrassment at the young man I had seen so briefly at Essex Grange. What had Flemynge called him? Aubrey Presscott.

'Mrs Flemynge?' he said, looking me up and down boldly and with evident surprise.

'How did you get in here?'

He smiled, and I thought: this is a man who believes himself to be irresistible to women. In fact, he was a very handsome man, slightly built, elegantly dressed, with crisp black hair brushed forward in fashionable curls.

'I came by way of the saloon, ma'am, not wishing to be announced. Don't blame Mrs Hobson for permitting it. She has had a . . . how shall I put it? . . . a weakness for me since she first came to Thorsby ten years ago.'

'How gallant of you to tell me, and how foolish. It may be necessary to find another housekeeper if Mrs Hobson forgets where her duty lies.'

The smile broadened. He was confident that I had no power in this house. 'Forgive me for startling you,' he said with a little lift of his hands, 'and I am sorry to learn that your husband has caused you so much suffering. I would not add to it for the world, because you *were* under the impression that I was Flemynge returned to you a moment ago, were you not? The man is a fool. I would never have left so great a beauty as you on the day after my wedding. The transformation, by the way, is breathtaking. I would not have known you for the same young person who stood so pathetically in the drawing-room of Essex Grange last week.'

'Yes,' I said as boldy as I could. 'We played a little trick on you.'

'Don't make me laugh, my dear. You had no part in the trick. You were a pawn.' And now the smile was gone. 'Flemynge is a villain. He has used you. Has it not occurred to you that you have now served your purpose? He may fling you out to fend for yourself or take you back to Chennings. It was all a waste of time, in any case. A drama, meant to upset my ailing father, and it did, of course. Poor Papa was ill for days. I say! He did *marry* you, didn't he? Are you certain of that?'

'Of course, I'm certain. The marriage lines are in my possession.'

'I only ask because rumour spoke of his unrequited love for an heiress in Suffolk. A Miss Makin. Her family did not approve, but that was all before Flemynge got his hands on Thorsby. A handsome estate can wipe out even the stigma of illegitimacy, I believe. So you see, you were quite a surprise to the gossips. Have you known your husband long? Did he conduct your courtship among the lunatics? I swear you could not have become quite so filthy, or forgive me, so odorous in a matter of days. How long were you an inmate?'

'That is none of your business. Anyway, I was committed improperly.'

'I believe you, Mrs Flemynge. Why should I not? But your husband did leave orders that you should not be allowed to leave the grounds of Thorsby. Now, why is that, I wonder?'

'His orders were a mistake, certainly, but he is a cautious man, wishing only for my well-being. I . . . supposing I had been indisposed, you can see that I am perfectly well now.' He smiled maddeningly. 'Well then, how does one prove one's sanity? If I asked you to *prove* you are sane, what would you do? What could you say to convince me?'

'Nothing,' he answered smoothly, humouring me. 'As you say, there is no way to prove one's sanity. I sympathize with your predicament. You may depend upon me. I shall tell everyone I meet that you show no more agitation than any other young woman would do who finds herself abandoned by her bridegroom and forbidden to leave his property in his absence. Shall we walk down to the stone bridge? I have a passion to see it once more. Are you allowed to go so far? So near to swiftly flowing water? But why not? I see no signs of instability. I am quite sure you have no desire to do away with yourself. You are, as you say, a sane and sensible woman, although your colour is a trifle high just at the moment.'

'What do you expect?' I asked. 'No woman wishes to hear her husband maligned.'

'Ah! Is that the reason? How affecting. You have mistaken him for a gentleman. But then, you don't know him very well do you? I suppose he is at pains to behave in a proper manner so long as he can control himself. Joanna Flemynge was a madcap, by all accounts. She had a fondness for gaming and men, you know. A reprehensible woman. You have been told, I suppose, that she and my father were husband and wife. It took an Act of Parliament and a fortune before Papa could free himself of her. Flemynge's father was my parent's fortune-hunting secretary. There is wildness on both sides. Flemynge must be afraid that at any moment, the evil blood of his parents will surface and cause him to take some rash, inexplicable action which he will later regret.'

'Mr Presscott, I have endured all I intend to from you. You are spiteful because you have lost Thorsby. Why don't you face the truth? Thorsby Hall belongs to Flemynge. Your father would never have moved away if he had known himself to be in the right.'

'My beloved father is senile,' said Aubrey Presscott bitterly. 'Had I known what was afoot, I would have come home from London and prevented him from leaving Thorsby at all costs. Make no mistake, however, I shall have this house one day. Then, and only then, Thorsby will be reunited with its treasures.'

I turned and started walking rapidly back to the house. A footman was running down the lawn towards us and I actually feared for a moment that he was going to scold me for going so far from the terrace. He had a different message, however.

'Mrs Flemynge. Some men with vans. Three furniture wagons.'

'But how extraordinary! They could not have made the furniture I ordered so soon.'

'Not that furniture, ma'am,' said the footman. 'Mr Flemynge's bought a whole houseful of furniture at an auction in Lincoln, it seems, and had it sent to Thorsby.'

'But he said *I* should furnish the family rooms,' I murmured. Aubrey Presscott laughed out loud.

We reached the hall in time to see the first heavy pieces set down by the sweating drovers. Settees, four of them, all in the most deplorable state of repair, were placed any which way on the marble floor. Grimed paintings by indifferent artists had already been stacked against one wall. An unsteady pedestal table stood drunkenly by the stairs, and the men were beginning to carry in a succession of dining chairs whose brown leather seats were, without exception, torn.

'Ah, I should have guessed that Flemynge was a man of exquisite taste,' said Mr Presscott. 'These settees will look magnificent in the saloon, don't you think? The faded green upholstery, just a trifle grubby here and there, will blend so nicely with the red brocade walls. And the van Dyck won't be missed when you hang this rather smaller painting of a girl and her dog. At least . . .' He looked at it critically. ' . . . I think that is what it is supposed to represent.'

I approached one of the removal men. 'Don't put these things in the hall. Take them all into the saloon, through that door. It will be the best place to keep it all until I can sort out which pieces must be burned or thrown away and which can be repaired.'

'The frugal housewife,' said Presscott, rummaging in a tea chest. 'I swear I have never seen chipped dinner plates at Thorsby in my entire life.'

I took the plate from Mr Presscott's hand and couldn't resist giving him a little push towards the door. 'Good day to you, sir. I'm afraid I'm going to be rather busy for the next few hours.'

I wanted nothing so much as to throw the plates – preferably at my husband – but I controlled my temper and directed the servants. Flemynge's brief note, which Grimsby remembered to give me half an hour later, explained that he had found the opportunity to buy up all the furniture of a Lincoln merchant in one job lot. Knowing the vast areas to be furnished, he hoped I would be able to salvage something to make me more comfortable until Thorsby's rightful furniture was returned. A sensible, even thoughtful, action on his part. But it was too late. I was in no mood to give my husband credit for anything, much less thoughtfulness.

Some of the furniture was decent enough. The dining chairs could be re-covered on the estate, I was told, and Jeb Marsden, one of my husband's tenants, could French polish the dining table in no time.

I added a few necessary items to my own room, then spitefully fitted out the bedchamber my husband used with all the most broken-down pieces of furniture I could possibly have an excuse to put into it. Finally, still angry, I had a brilliant idea of how to annoy him.

The servants went about following my orders quickly and efficiently, but they looked doubtful when told that I intended to have a joke at the expense of the master of the house.

Within an hour, everything was in place. A small faded carpet, about nine feet square, lay in the very middle of the saloon like a napkin attempting to clothe a banqueting table. Two settees of uncertain years had been placed on the carpet with great care for symmetry, their sagging seats facing each other across the space of five feet or so. Each was guarded at the back by a mahogany sofa table which held matching oil lamps with green shades. Lined up at right angles to the settees on the very edge of the carpet – for I would allow nothing to touch the floor – was a small escritoire. The rest of the room was completely bare as it had been when I first arrived, except for a selection of the worst paintings I could find. The effect was ludicrous.

For days I tested out possible answers to Flemynge's inevitable questions about the saloon: I thought he wished me to do the best I could with whatever was to hand, or I thought this furniture was representative of his taste, or better still, he clearly didn't trust *me* to purchase any furniture, so what else was I to do? All of these ripostes lacked a cutting edge and, furthermore, depended on his asking the right question. I was beginning to tire of the joke and wished I hadn't thought of it in the first place.

The irony was, I spent one afternoon sitting in the saloon and found the arrangement amazingly comfortable. The room was cool and airy and the view from the windows the most pleasing in the house. An hour later I moved my novels, needlework and watercolours into the saloon and, to the obvious disapproval of Mrs Hobson, made myself at home.

On the fifteenth day, the first of the furnishings I had ordered was delivered: a settee which I had chosen from Mr Hope's *Household Furniture and Decoration*. Naturally, I had not ordered the settee from the great Mr Hope, himself, but from a less expensive local cabinet maker who had promised speedy delivery.

When the settee was carried into the morning-room by two sweating servants, I could have wept. What had seemed dramatic, modern and in perfect taste in the drawing, had been translated into a grotesque piece of furniture which was heavy, ostentatious and totally out of keeping with the other items in the room. Worse, it was uncomfortable.

It had no back, but it did have raised square cushions at each end which might take a cautious elbow. I say cautious, because each of these cushions was guarded front and back by raised wooden boxes topped by no less than four carved black sphinxes, glaring at one another across the seat. The Thing (I refused to think of it as a settee) had heavy stubby legs and was upholstered in virulent green and white stripes.

Briefly, I considered having it carried to my own chamber where Flemynge would never see it, but immediately discarded the idea. It had been outrageously expensive and the bill for it would arrive on Mr Stornaway's desk in due course. Flemynge would be bound to hear of it. So I allowed it to remain in the morning-room where it reminded me of my folly every time I looked at it.

On the sixteenth day, Flemynge returned home and caught me unawares attempting to find a comfortable position on the Thing. I jumped up in embarrassment, caught my elbow on a sphinx and let out a cry of pain. It was not the homecoming I had planned for him.

# Chapter Four

'So you have returned at last,' I said, rubbing my elbow.

Flemynge looked past me at the Thing. 'Yes. You seem to have filled out since I last saw you.'

'I've become fat, do you mean?'

'I mean that the dark circles have disappeared from beneath your eyes and there are no longer hollows in your cheeks. And your gown is of the first stare. I'm pleased to see my wife looking so fashionable.' Flemynge continued to regard the settee, but was aware apparently that the butler had entered the room. 'You may dish me up some grilled kidneys, if you have any, Grimsby, and some of your excellent coffee. Have you finished your breakfast, Elinor? Have another cup of coffee, anyway.'

'When did you return?'

'Late last night. In fact, after one o'clock this morning.'

I gestured towards the settee. 'Since you have not taken your eyes off it, you may as well say what you are thinking.'

He looked at me, then, smiling slightly. 'It's hideous.'

'I know, but at least it is sound. Not like the furniture you bought in Lincolnshire. Don't you think you could have had the courtesy to tell me why you were going away and how long you would be gone?'

'Forgive me.' He sat down and began to eat his breakfast. 'The estate contained some unentailed property in York that I decided to sell. I may add some acres to the home farm, I haven't made up my mind yet. Or I may invest the money. In any case, I have no interest in owning a mill in York. I don't know anything about farms, either.' He grinned. 'To tell you the truth, since we hardly know each other, I hadn't thought you would care where I went, or how long I stayed away.'

'I don't. You may go to the devil for all I care.'

Flemynge looked up at the butler who was standing at attention by the sideborad, and waved him out of the room.

I was silent following my childish outburst. I drank my coffee, wondering how the conduct of this meeting, this confrontation, had slipped from my grasp. I had known exactly what I wanted to say to him, but now couldn't manage to speak at all.

He finished his kidneys and two slices of toast before looking up at me. 'We must discuss your estate, Elinor. I will see to it that my lawyer writes to your aunt demanding your inheritance.'

'Yes.' I was stunned. 'Yes, it is very good of you to concern yourself, but my uncle seemed to be in serious debt when he took me to Chennings. I don't have much hope of regaining anything.'

'Nevertheless, we must try. Now then.' He put his napkin on the table and stood up. 'Shall we go into the saloon?'

'You know about the saloon?' I murmured in embarrassment. He was already at the door, holding it open for me, still smiling. I was beginning to wish he would show a little healthy, normal anger.

'Caxton warned me this morning, so I went to the saloon to see what you had ordered to be done before joining you in the morning-room.'

'I can explain —'

'I think it a charming conceit. Why not enjoy the room? It may be some time before the legal battle is over and we have Thorsby's original contents in place.' He opened the door to the saloon and ushered me in. My well-practised phrases remained unspoken as we sat down facing one another, I nervously perched on the edge of my settee; he, perfectly at his ease as he lounged back in his.

'Yes,' he said at last. 'Very comfortable. You did well to arrange this furniture here. I am delighted that you have made yourself at home.'

I felt amazingly uncomfortable, but Flemynge appeared not to notice as he turned slightly to remove a large blue velvet box from the table behind him. The box had certainly not been there on the previous evening, so I presumed he had placed it on the table that morning.

'This box requires some explanation, I think.' Thoughtfully, he caressed the velvet with his thumb, before looking up at me. 'When my mother fled with her ... with my father from this house, she took with her only the parure which had been her wedding present from my grandfather. She had intended to sell it, but after my father died, decided that by rights it belonged to me, to be given to my wife. Over the years, I came to hate this set of jewels, feeling that the money they would have fetched could have set me on a different path. However, things have a way of working out for the best. Today, I am able to give them to you not only as a bride present but also as a gift for your twenty-first birthday.' He opened the box to reveal a magnificent emerald and diamond necklace with matching earrings and bracelet. 'Isn't it fortunate that emeralds will suit you so well?'

He stood up to hand them to me, then sat down beside me as I tried to find the words to thank him. I felt perfectly wretched and could not prevent the tears from welling up into my eyes.

'I . . . I have no right –' I stammered.

'You have every right to them. You are my wife. I hope you will be very happy here, Elinor.'

I picked up the bracelet and held it to one wrist. Immediately, Flemynge reached forward to close the clasp.

'I have been poor company, for which I must apologize,' he said. 'However, it is a beautiful day and I have no commitments this afternoon. Would you care to go for a drive?'

'You have a racing curricle,' I said. 'I've seen it in the stables. Will you take me for a ride in it?'

'We will ride in my curricle. Do you drive?'

'I'm reckoned to be a fair whip,' I said, which had not been at all my uncle's opinion.

'In that case, I will let you take the reins for a short spell.'

Flemynge stood up and so did I, holding out my wrist for him to remove the bracelet. I couldn't look directly at him. 'I believe there is a place not too far from here called High Beech. I should like to drive there.'

'I don't suppose there is anything remarkable about High Beech, but we can certainly drive through it. This afternoon at two o'clock? I will meet you here in the saloon. But Elinor, I have just one favour to ask of you. I know I said that I would never ask another after our visit to Essex Grange, but this is rather different.'

'Of course!' I cried. 'Anything I can do to –'

'I do not want you to read novels in future.'

I gaped at him. 'But everyone reads novels! I don't read *French* novels, if that is what you mean.'

'I mean any sort of novel. Obey me in this, Elinor. Novels excite the imagination. I believe them to be lowering to the mind. There are many other books in this house that will improve your understanding. Will you do as I ask?'

He had been so kind to me this morning that I couldn't bring myself to argue with him. I nodded without saying anything, and left the room.

The years spent living in my uncle's house had taught me something of the ways of men. So long as they were not openly challenged, so long as one maintained a meek attitude, they seldom investigated to see if their strictures were being obeyed. I, therefore, went to my room there and then. Having hidden three unread novels in a hatbox, I sat down by the window and read until twelve, finishing the three-volume novel I had been reading since the beginning of the week just before a plate of ham and a glass of wine were brought to my room by Millichip.

By two o'clock I was dressed in a carriage gown of yellow silk with a yellow-ribboned straw bonnet tied firmly over my short curls. I took up the novel I had just finished and went downstairs to the saloon where I placed the books with a flourish on one of the tables.

'You may wish to take charge of these,' I said sweetly and I could see that Flemynge was impressed.

'Stornaway tells me High Beech has nothing to recommend it except an ancient inn. We must see what the view is like.'

It was bliss to be bowling along in an open carriage. Flemynge allowed me to tool the horse between Theydon Green and the Wake Arms, but I could see that he was not easy about it. Taking the reins from me as we turned left by the old inn, he said: 'Well done,' without enthusiasm. He was, I had to admit, an expert whip, one not given to taking foolish chances. He was a cautious man who knew his own skills and the capabilities of his animal to an inch.

I could appreciate his talent as I sat beside him, but it didn't change my view of him as a husband. He would find he could not drive me so skilfully.

High fluffy clouds had tracked us all the way so far, but when we entered Epping Forest, the trees closed overhead to give us some relief from the sun's relentless rays. There wasn't a breath of air except what our brisk pace stirred up, and the stillness had a magical quality. The road was empty, but I occasionally caught a glimpse of a family silently, intently, gathering firewood beneath the trees. Even the youngest child had a bundle on his back. The noise of horse and carriage disturbed the birds from time to time, and Flemynge solemnly named them for me.

We had been travelling for almost an hour and the horse was beginning to tire as we took the steep climb to Royal Oak Hill.

'I want to stop here for a few minutes so that we can look round,' said Flemynge.

My heart began to beat fiercely. The Royal Oak Inn was just a few yards away, now framed by trees in full leaf and looking less bleak than when I had last seen it. I licked my lips and couldn't resist straightening the bow on my bonnet.

A superb stand of white-barked birch trees prevented us from appreciating what would otherwise have been a splendid view of the valley. After a few minutes, Flemynge said we should move along to view the church. I nodded, incapable of speech, seeing nothing, really, except the inn, its many gables and diamond-paned windows, its stuccoed walls and red-tiled roof.

Was *he* in one of those cool rooms? Might he not stroll out to sit on the bench in front of the inn with the other men, a clay pipe between his lips, a tankard in his hand? But no, we passed the Royal Oak at a trot. No one started up in surprise at the sight of me. No one waved us to a halt.

When we were well past the inn, Flemynge whipped up the horse and we moved off smartly towards the church which stood in the depths of woodland without a house in sight. It was an attractive old building of grey stone with a lych-gate, yew trees and a sprinkling of gravestones.

Flemynge dismounted to tie up the horse and bait him, while I climbed down unaided. A little distance away the woodland beckoned; well-spaced beech trees with trunks gnarled about eight feet up, and sturdy branches reaching skywards. Fan vaulting in nature's cathedral, I thought. The ground was almost covered with dead brown beech leaves which crunched underfoot as I made my way over the little valleys and mossy mounds. Tree trunks were dusted with brilliant green on their north sides, and here and there bare earth was seeded with large pebbles like a child's mud pudding. Just then a shaft of light penetrated the dense shadow to nourish one small corner of the dead earth. I ran forward with a cry and sank to my knees in the light of the sun.

'Elinor!'

'It's so beautiful, it reminds me of the good days, before my parents died. I'm sorry, Flemynge. You don't like tears. I shall control myself in a minute, but, you see, I had almost forgotten. The Old Manor House is just outside Cheltenham, and it is surrounded by beech woods. We used to go for walks there when I was a little girl. Later, I felt myself to be town bred and would have nothing to do with trees and flowers.' I reached out to touch several small white-petalled cups alternating up a spindly stem. 'Look! White helleborine. I used to . . .' Tears thickened my voice. I rummaged blindly in my pocket for a handkerchief.

'Sudden memories of childhood can be distressingly potent,' he said quietly. 'We'll have our picnic here on this mound, shall we? I'll fetch the rug and the basket. No, don't get up. Stay where you are.'

By the time he had returned and spread the thick fur rug on the ground, I was quite recovered, grateful for his sensitivity in allowing me time to get my emotions under control.

Chef had packed lemonade and fruit cake, napkins and serviceable china – the very pieces that I had first seen among the furniture from Lincoln. Flemynge poured the lemonade into pewter tankards while I cut the cake and placed a slice on each plate, rescuing all the raisins that fell onto the rug and eating them like a child.

'Was there ever anything so marvellous as to sit in the dark woods and have a picnic on a fur rug?' I asked. 'The lemonade is very cold.'

'I have eaten many a meal in the open air, sometimes

cooking my food over a small fire. I always found that food tastes better that way and that I have a greater appetite than ever I do in a dining-room.' He reached out idly to point to a leafy plant that had found enough light in which to grow. 'Lords and ladies. Perhaps you call it Jack-in-the-pulpit. Do you know its proper name? *Arum maculatum*. And here –'

'Flemynge, why does Mr Stornaway persist in saying that there is no inventory for Thorsby?'

'He insists that he has never seen one.'

'And do you believe him?'

'Of course not. Hold out your tankard and I will pour you some more lemonade.'

'I have been thinking about the problem. Take care! You're spilling it.'

'There is no need for you to get involved. I have a lawyer whose task it is to worry about my affairs.'

'Didn't you tell me that an uncle of yours advised you to claim the house? Why not write to him and ask if *he* has a record of Thorsby's more important possessions? The house isn't that old. What would you say, less than a hundred years? Either the better paintings and *objets* have been in your mother's family for a generation or more, or they were purchased more recently. He should be able to tell you one way or the other. The previous land steward is bound to have kept receipts and records, perhaps of restoration or repairs.'

'What a good idea! That's very clever of you, Elinor!'

'And you thought me a dimwit,' I teased.

He denied it so vehemently and with such seriousness that it quite spoiled my good mood. I helped myself to another piece of cake and turned my back on him to look deep into the woods.

'Don't sulk, Elinor, I didn't mean to offend you.'

'I never sulk.'

'I am surprised to hear it,' he laughed.

I twisted round to look at him. 'We could sneak into

Stornaway's office at dead of night and go through his papers.'

'There's no need for stealth. I have a right to look at anything I please. It's my house now, although I think Stornaway needs reminding of that from time to time.'

'But of course stealth is necessary. What a poor conspirator you make. We must not arouse his suspicions, you see. He must not know what we are doing, lest he destroy everything.'

'A lurid suggestion. Now you see why I object to the reading of novels.'

I let the remark pass unchallenged.

'You didn't hear a word I said, did you?' he asked after a slight pause.

I caught the serious note in his voice and was at once contrite. 'About reading novels? Oh yes, Flemynge, I did, I assure you.'

'No, about the plant, lords and ladies. I was telling you about its proper name.'

'We used to call it cuckoo pint.'

'That illustrates the point I want to make. Two people in different parts of the world, perhaps speaking different languages, and wishing to discuss this plant, might call it by two different names. It is necessary to have one name which is universally known.'

'Do they have cuckoo pints all over the world?'

'No.'

'Well, then. The problem does not exist,' I said, but he pressed on.

'A Swede named Carl Linné published a brilliant book in 1753 giving Latin names to thousands of plants found all over the world. He used two words to describe each one. They are the genus name and the specific name. Your cuckoo pint and my lords and ladies is called *Arum maculatum* by Linné, or Linnaeus as we call him now. *Arum* is the genus and this plant is specifically *maculatum*, which means spotted. See the spots on the leaves?'

To tell the truth, I thought he was a trifle eccentric and *very* boring. Nevertheless, I dutifully bent forward and observed the brownish spots on the arrow-head leaves at the base of the plant. 'So, anywhere in the world people will call this plant *Arum* and a word meaning spotted?'

'*Arum maculatum*, yes.'

'Can you name every plant in this wood?' I asked, teasing him.

'Not much grows at this time of year under beech trees because of the dense shade, but yes, I can. That bramble patch is *Rubus fructicosus*, and there is *Ilex aquifolium*.'

'That's holly!'

'Yes, and the common beech is *Fagus sylvaticus*.'

I was impressed in spite of myself. 'How clever you are, Flemynge. But how can you remember so many names?'

'It is not as difficult as you might imagine. You could learn if you would try. It would exercise your mind. And when the autumn comes, we can return here and see how many toadstools we can discover. They, too, have been named, you know.'

I had been looking about for a way to bring him down. 'And pray, sir, what is this?'

'I can't tell from here.'

'Oh, come now, Flemynge. It's moss!'

'Yes, of course it's moss, but I can't tell what sort from this distance. Dig up a piece and hand it to me.'

I dug my nails into the vivid green mound and handed a small clump across the rug. 'Do you mean to say that there are several different kinds of moss?'

'Quite a few, yes. Essex is a dry county and so the variety of mosses is not so great as in other places. Wales and the Lakes are better habitats. I will have to consult my books.'

I laughed. 'Are you not afraid that in examining everything in nature so closely you will fail to appreciate its beauty? Not seeing the wood for the trees, as it were. In putting a Latin label to something so small, have you not failed to appreciate the brilliant green velvet bed that it makes with its fellows?'

'No, I think that those who don't look at nature so closely as I do fail to appreciate the glory of God. He made each small tuft of moss. We should not forget it. But, I'm sorry, I'm boring you.'

'Never! Do tell me more.'

He missed the sarcasm. 'Well, let me see, Linnaeus tried to sort out the natural order of plants, or at least to devise a better system of categorizing them than others had done. He introduced a sexual system of grouping them –'

'Now you are teasing me.'

'No, I assure you. He noted the reproductive parts of flowers – the female ovaries which are called styles and the male organs which are called stamens, and used this form of identification as a means of placing plants into families.'

Stretching out, he pulled up the lords and ladies and moved closer. 'This is the spathe. It's like a leaf, only much paler, and it makes the pulpit for Jack.'

I don't know what possessed me, but I pointed to the purplish stalk in the middle, now slightly drooping, and gave him an arch look. 'And which part is that, the male part or the female part?'

He flushed. 'Neither. Try to pay attention to what I am saying instead of sniggering like a boy of ten. This part which is supposed to be Jack of Jack-in-the-pulpit and looks a bit like a small bullrush, is the flower head or spadix. Now, below it – do you see?' He pulled away the spathe and dropped it on the rug. 'On the stem of the spadix is a ring of hairs pointing downwards. Below that are the male flowers and below them the female flowers.'

'How disappointing,' I said crisply. 'Both sexes on the same plant.'

He gave me a stern look. 'Insects are attracted to the plant and crawl inside. Once they have passed below the hairs, they cannot get out. They crawl over the male flowers, picking up pollen. Then they crawl over the female flowers, completing pollination.'

'So that is where babies come from!'

He stood up and tossed the plant parts to the ground. 'Never have I met such an irritating, frivolous, indelicate female.'

'That's unfair! It was you who brought up the subject. It sounds fantastic to me. I'm not sure you didn't make it up just to embarrass me. It was not a suitable topic of conversation. And even if all this is true, I'm sure I am not the first person to say so.'

'Women of intelligence and breeding all over the world have taken an interest in botany without once entertaining the lewd thoughts that spring so naturally to your mind.' He pointed to the scattered parts of the *Arum*. 'That was my life for many years.'

'What? Determining the sex of plants? How erotic!'

'I meant botany . . . plant hunting. I went to New Holland with . . . oh, what the devil does it matter?'

Drawing up my knees to hug them as I sat on the rug, I said in a mocking voice: 'Elinor is a naughty ten-year-old boy. Elinor must not tease her husband, because he has no sense of humour.'

'I do! But I suppose I cannot see the joke, which was more suited to the smoking-room, anyway. You ridicule the science that was for so long the source of my happiness. A boy of no education has few chances to leave home and lead a life of adventure in the company of cultured men. My interest in and knowledge of plants enabled me to take up the post of assistant to a botanist who was going on an expedition to the Antipodes. You think me humourless; I think you are . . . oh, never mind.'

Angrily, I began to gather the picnic things into the

basket, annoyed when he bent to help. We didn't speak again until we were back in the carriage and well on our way.

'It is essential that you find some worthwhile employment, Elinor. I will not have you idling away the days. Obviously, you cannot bring yourself to take an interest in plants the way I do. However, I gather that you paint in water colours.'

'Painting is to me what botany is to you,' I said simply.

'In that case, perhaps you would paint some pictures of garden plants at Thorsby. There are some rare specimens in the grounds and I would like to have a record of them. I will show you which ones I mean when we arrive home.'

I recognized an olive branch when I saw one, and grasped it eagerly. 'Oh, I should love to! Yes, that would be a splendid idea. You won't be disappointed, but I will need some more paints and a better quality paper.'

'We will drive into Chelmsford tomorrow so that you can purchase your supplies.'

'Oh, Flemynge, that reminds me! The servants seem to think that you had forbidden me to leave the grounds of Thorsby. And Mr Stornaway refused to take what he called the *responsibility* for driving me into Chelmsford so that I could make some purchases on my own behalf. It has been extremely galling.'

I looked at him as I spoke and noticed a small tightening of the muscles in his jaw.

'You didn't give such an order, did you?'

For several seconds, he said nothing. The stillness of the forest began to oppress me, the only sound being the steady hoofbeats of our horse.

'Elinor, it may have been that they misunderstood my purpose. I am hated by the friends of the Presscotts. You might have received a number of hurtful snubs. I wished to prevent that.'

'The servants think I am mad. In fact, I'm sure that for miles around the gossips are enjoying themselves with tales of the mad mistress of Thorsby. That is your fault, Flemynge, for taking me to Essex Grange that day. It is not too late to mend matters, however. You must let it be known that I was committed improperly, that you have not really married a madwoman.'

He said nothing, nor did he even glance in my direction. As the silence lengthened, I had to accept that he, too, thought me mad. Yet, I could have sworn that he hadn't thought so on our wedding day. What could possibly have happened in the past sixteen days to change his mind?

Now that I seriously considered the matter, I realized that he had behaved quite differently towards me all day. On our wedding day, he had spoken of the injustices of my committal. On this day there had been no mention of injustice.

'While you were away, did you visit Chennings again?' I asked.

'Of course not. I told you I went to York and that is the truth.'

'You are like all the rest,' I accused. 'You also think I'm mad.'

'No, I do not. I do believe you have suffered a great deal in the past few months, enough to try any young woman's nerves. I simply want you to rest and gain strength. Be guided by me, Elinor.'

'Have I any choice?' I asked bitterly.

He smiled in that odiously superior manner that he had been using towards me all day, and gave my hands a patronizing pat as they lay in my lap. In future, I saw, he would treat me politely but distantly, and he would watch me all the time, just as the servants had been doing. My every word and action would be noted and misinterpreted.

No longer was I in any doubt about my future. The

decision had been taken for me. I would have to swallow my pride and contact Tad immediately. Furthermore, he would have to be told that I had no fortune, nor any prospect of one, because my property was not protected by entailment. Whatever Flemynge succeeded in wresting from my aunt would belong to him as my lawful husband.

To add to my growing depression, doubts about Tad began to assail me. Was he, in fact, a fortune-hunter? Blinking back my tears, I thought about the letter I would send to the Royal Oak. I would say only that my uncle was dead and that I was now residing at Thorsby Hall. I would simply ask Tad to fetch me. Time enough to tell him about my inheritance when we were reunited.

Posting the letter could be difficult, but I thought I could manage to outwit Grimsby and hand the letter directly to the postman when he called.

I looked once more at Flemynge's uncompromising profile and thought about what might have been: a life of ease at Thorsby Hall, position, wealth, security; a perfect existence marred only occasionally by a botanical lecture.

Instead, in the course of what I hoped would be a short marriage, I was to be given diamond and emerald necklaces but refused novels, allowed to paint but forbidden to walk in the village unattended. Flemynge had held out the illusion of freedom, only to imprison me in a different way, calling forth my gratitude by giving me expensive gifts and so stifling my rebellion. Mr McCann had been a much less complicated jailor.

Flemynge glanced down as I was wiping the tears from my cheeks. 'You are tired, my dear.'

'Yes, Flemynge,' I said wearily. 'I find that life itself is tiring.'

# Chapter Five

I began to paint like someone possessed, turning all my energies and thoughts towards producing work that would dazzle Flemynge. *Elinor*, he would say, *I never dreamed you had such talent! These paintings are magnificent! I must arrange for you to have a private exhibition.*

Buoyed up by these ridiculous daydreams and tired out each day by the hours spent at my easel, I was able to thrust Tad to the back of my mind. I had managed to send a letter to him, but had no idea how long it would be before he arrived at Thorsby. Counting the minutes, the hours, the days would drive me to distraction. Much better to take up every waking moment with painting and, of course, with a determined effort to appear sane and responsible.

Flemynge was not at all helpful in this direction. He treated me with such kindness and consideration, such formal concern for my health, that he succeeded in making me very irritable. Yet, if I gave a sharp answer to one of his endless queries about my well-being, I invariably ended by apologizing profusely, lest he have further cause to think me mentally unsound. I never left the estate alone, but he was always ready to take me for long walks in and around the village, or on rides further afield.

I soon lost interest in walking in the immediate neighbourhood. The natives, rich and poor, treated us as if we were from another civilization, and stood gawping long after we had passed. I once turned round suddenly and caught them at it, but Flemynge told me not to do so again. Nevertheless, I think he found their curiosity as galling as I did.

About a week after his return from York, I was seated under a tree by the old stone bridge, attempting to capture the sparkle of light upon the small stream that ran sluggishly beneath it, when I looked up to see a footman heading towards me.

'Sir Hesketh and Lady Maltby have come to call,' said the young lad, 'and master sent me to fetch you to the saloon.'

'The saloon?' I asked dumbly. 'He is entertaining them in the *saloon*?'

'Yes, ma'am.'

Nervously, I removed my painting apron and dropped it on the ground, finger-combed what was left of my hair and began to walk back towards the house, with the servant a few paces behind me.

'John,' I said, turning suddenly. 'Who are the Maltbys?'

'Estate next to Thorsby. Only small, not a decent-sized room in the house, so I'm told, but the Maltbys have been there for a long time and are very well liked, I believe. They have a daughter, ma'am, who has come with them. Very – They are your nearest neighbours,' he ended abruptly.

I could see he felt embarrassed by having spoken so much, so I didn't question him further.

Just then, Flemynge and our guests walked out on to the terrace, and I had a chance to see for myself what the footman couldn't bring himself to say. The daughter was exquisite. She was about my age, I thought, with glorious golden hair and pale porcelain skin. I was beginning to hope that she and I might become firm friends, when she turned to look at me, and I was struck by her remarkably vacant expression. Or perhaps this was the look she wore when about to meet a madwoman.

Flemynge came down the shallow terrace steps to take me by the arm. 'May I present my bride? Elinor, Sir

Hesketh and Lady Maltby and their daughter, Miss Clarissa Maltby, have come to call on us.'

'We are your neighbours,' said Sir Hesketh. 'Albany House, you know.' He pointed vaguely towards our western boundary. He was about fifty, a man who obviously took infinite pains over his appearance, seemingly anxious to fight off the encroaching years. I categorized him as a rattle with very little else but dress on his mind.

His wife smiled at me in a friendly, encouraging way and I found her more to my taste: attractive, bright-eyed, intelligent. She, too, was very smartly dressed, and I supposed that clothing played an important part in her life also.

The daughter must, therefore, be something of a disappointment to them. Her hand in mine was limp and slightly damp. Her extraordinary features showed little animation, and her over-decorated, crumpled gown sat badly on her. There are some women who cannot successfully wear even the most delightful gowns, and Clarissa Maltby was one of them.

There was some indecision about where we might all sit, which was settled for us by Clarissa. The terrace was too hot, she said in her rather whiny voice, and the sun hurt her eyes. It was just as well, I supposed, since there were only two stone benches on the terrace, and they were permanently fixed several yards apart.

We returned to the saloon and I was amused to see these fine people trying to settle themselves comfortably on the shabby furniture, while attempting not to notice the peculiar arrangement of the vast room. I caught a glimpse of Flemynge's face and saw that he, too, found it amusing. I was inclined to think that my husband had no sense of humour, and certainly no sense of the ridiculous, but he had surprised me in that direction on one or two occasions.

'My dear fellow, you must forgive us for not calling

sooner,' said Sir Hesketh. 'It's been a trifle awkward, you know. The Presscotts are friends of ours. We have seen them several times a week since our marriage twenty-five years ago.'

I found this candid remark quite disarming, but couldn't resist saying: 'And what do you think of your friends' behaviour in stealing our furniture?'

'Too bad, I'm sure,' said Lady Maltby quickly. Wearing a wry smile, she indicated the entire room with a sweep of her arm. 'But you have contrived magnificently.'

Flemynge and I both laughed. 'Thank you,' I said. 'Having seen this example of our taste, you won't be surprised to hear we plan to keep pigs in the ballroom'.

'A splendid idea, my dear,' said Lady Maltby. 'And the only suitable use for that abominable floor. I'm sure the pigs will dance more gracefully on it than I ever could.'

'I furnished the saloon in this fashion to show how impossible it is to replace the proper furniture by other purchases,' I explained, and added mischievously, 'And also because I thought it would annoy my husband.'

'An important consideration for any bride,' replied Lady Maltby drily as the men laughed. 'Start as you mean to go on. Correct me if I'm wrong, Mrs Flemynge,' she added, 'but are you, by any chance, a painter?'

'Yes, how —'

'There's green paint on your nose,' said Flemynge. I shot him a malevolent look. 'I didn't tell you before because I think it suits you very well.'

I ignored him, rubbing my nose vigorously. 'I was out of doors painting when you arrived, Lady Maltby. Would you and your daughter care to take a turn in the garden? It's such a beautiful day.'

Lady Maltby rose at once. 'That would be very pleasant. Come, Clarissa,' she added in a whisper, 'and try, my dear, not to monopolize the conversation.'

A dull stain crept up Clarissa's neck. 'I have nothing to say, Mama,' she murmured as we left the saloon for the garden, which Lady Maltby said always looked its very best at the height of summer.

We walked down to the bridge, where Lady Maltby examined the water colour on my easel. 'But you really are very good, my dear! Were you taught or is this just natural talent?'

'I had several good art masters. It was the one subject I enjoyed.'

'I don't believe I know your maiden name, Mrs Flemynge.'

I knew at once what information Lady Maltby was seeking.

'Burns-Roberts. You wouldn't know the family. They were merchants in the City. I lived with my aunt and uncle until I went to Chennings.'

'No, I don't suppose I have heard of the family. Perhaps Hildebrand Presscott might . . . Oh, dear. I didn't intend to mention his name. However, I must ask you. Does Mr Flemynge ever speak of his mother?'

'Occasionally. I believe he quite despised her.'

'Oh, do beware of men who claim to hate their mothers! They make abominable husbands. Their poor wives must never do those things which they disliked in their mamas. But mark my words, there always turns out to be some quite surprising little trait which they positively demand in the woman they've married.'

Lady Maltby leant her elbows on the bridge wall and looked into the water. 'Joanna and her son were together too much, I expect. A man should never see too much of his mother. My mama-in-law understands this perfectly. Dear Maltby and his mother once attended the same ball and didn't recognize one another until the evening was half over. So, you see, I have no problems about his hating his mother; he doesn't know her well enough to form an opinion. He hates *my* mother, of course, but that's a different matter.'

She plucked a leaf from a nearby tree and tossed it into the stream. 'Your husband must be very pleased to have so talented a wife.'

'He hasn't seen any of my work yet. It's to be a surprise when I have finished a set of six flower paintings.'

'How sweet! I am sure yours is a love match. If I may, as an older woman, give you some advice . . . You should learn all you can about your mother-in-law. In your case, it will be the key to happiness.'

'Marriage is extraordinarily difficult, isn't it?'

'An impossible state of affairs, but essential for the weaker sex. I always feel, don't you, that one relies on one's mate to provide that which one's parents failed to give. Or in Maltby's case, what his nanny failed to give him.'

'That is certainly an original thought,' I said. 'However, I can't think of anything my parents failed to give me. They were wonderful. They died when I was only fourteen and since then I have been terribly lonely.'

'There you are! You are looking for companionship in your marriage. For my part, my mother would never listen to anything I said. Maltby, on the other hand, attends to every word. That is why I vowed, when Clarissa was born, that if she ever said anything of interest, I would listen most carefully.'

To draw attention away from the blushing girl, I said: 'Tell me, Lady Maltby, did you ever meet my mother-in-law?'

'I knew her in the first year of her marriage. There wasn't a second year, of course. A most impulsive woman.'

'Was she a beauty?'

'She was an heiress. Beauty was not required of her.'

'And . . . I don't suppose you ever met my husband's father.'

'Fitzroy Buckland? Yes, I saw him once or twice. You would not have liked him, I promise you. An odious little time-server, all but wringing his hands in the presence of his employer, then servicing Joanna whenever Hildebrand's back was turned. I beg your pardon! That was a trifle too warm. Clarissa, pretend you didn't hear me speak.'

The Maltby's visit lasted for the correct twenty minutes. When we had seen them into their carriage, I turned to Flemynge.

'Our first visitors. They don't seem to feel superior to us or to dislike us.'

'No. As a matter of fact, they came to invite us to their summer ball next week. It is short notice, but they could hardly have invited us sooner. Besides, I think Sir Hesketh had to do a little soul searching before abandoning his old friends in favour of the new owner of Thorsby. I accepted the invitation, of course.'

'Yes, you had no choice if you . . . *we* are to become established. But I am a little nervous. We are both hated hereabouts, I think.'

'Possibly. You must order a gown immediately, and you will wear the emeralds. You are an exceptionally beautiful woman, Elinor. It goes without saying that every woman present will hate you. As for the men, they will hate me for having seen you first.'

This was such a pretty speech, that I was thrown into confusion. 'More beautiful than Miss Makin?' I asked stupidly.

'Miss Makin was not particularly beautiful. Who told you about her?'

'Mr Aubrey Presscott called while you were away. Flemynge, I'm sorry. I should not have mentioned her –'

'No, but you *should* have told me about Presscott. Why did you allow him into the house? Have you no sense?'

'No, I . . . Mrs Hobson let him in. I was standing on

the terrace and he suddenly appeared beside me. He said horrid things to me and I sent him packing.'

'As I shall do to Mrs Hobson.'

'No! What would we do without her? I can't manage this house . . . Besides, what if . . . Wait until later. Who can say what will happen in the future?'

'Who, indeed?' he said with surprising bitterness, and walked away.

Two days after the Maltby's visit, I laid my collection of six paintings one by one on a large piece of card which I had placed on my bed. First, Hume's Blush tea-scented China rose – an ugly white thing on a weak stem. For some reason that had not been explained to me, this plant had to be grown in the conservatory. I had been forced to spend several hours in the glaring heat to paint it, which had given me a headache.

With its strangely high-centred blooms, its floppy neck and susceptibility to cold winds, Hume's Blush was a sad bush, and I had chosen to emphasize this head-hanging quality. The idea had not been entirely successful. I decided to show Flemynge this one last.

Next came the *Colutea arborescens* – small yellow flowers which did not inspire me.

On top of this, I placed the honeysuckle, a plant I loved and fancied I had caught very well. A butterfly hovered above the flowers, improving the composition. In so far as I had confidence in any of my work, I felt confident of this one.

I had never heard of *Kalmia latifolia*, so it was rather interesting to try to capture it on paper. The shrub was small with glossy leaves, and bore heads of twenty or more little pink cups with yellow centres. I had managed to express the delicacy of the plant, and its strangeness. One of my better paintings.

I had also painted the white many-petalled rose, *Rosa centifolia muscosa alba*, as Flemynge insisted on calling it, only the day before. Flemynge should be impressed: I was myself and placed it second.

It occurred to me that I had been accustomed in the past merely to dabble at painting. As a girl, I had dedicated my life to being bored, to refusing to try to achieve anything. The present Elinor would have been inclined to give the young Elinor a good shake, and then I remembered my aunt had done just that on several occasions.

I wiped my hands down the sides of my gown before picking up the last painting. My little masterpiece: the passion flower. The blooms on the vine were so intricate, so delicately shaded, yet garish in their contrasts, that I had known at once this would be the greatest challenge. Everything had worked out just as I had planned – several enormous blooms crowding the page, misty and ill-defined, dripping with emotion. I was aware of the symbolism of the Crucifixion in the flower, and had tried to put something of my own tumultuous emotions on the paper. I squared the painting with the others, gave it a superstitious pat and covered them all with tissue.

These six pictures marked a change in my attitude to life and to painting. It was important that they should meet with Flemynge's approval. I had tried hard, thought about each one and how I was going to approach the subject. There had been dozens of false starts. Flemynge *must* be impressed, because so much depended on it. When he had seen and marvelled at these pictures, he would no longer treat me as an ailing idiot. He would respect my talent and, it followed, me.

'Are you ready?' I asked a few minutes later, as I stood at the doorway of the library.

Flemynge was seated behind a large desk with several heavy books open before him. I had discovered the secret of the stacks of books on the floor. He pressed plants between sheets of blotting paper, draining away their colour and squeezing out their life's juices by putting books on top of them to act as weights – *peine forte et dure*.

'Flemynge! Are you ready?'

He looked up, laying aside his magnifying glass. 'Yes, I've just been looking at some drawings done many years ago. You have your paintings with you? Come over here where the light is better.'

He began closing the books and stacking them to one side to make room for my work. He was dressed in breeches and wore his shirt open at the throat on this warm day. His sleeves were turned up several times, baring his forearms the way I preferred to see him. I thought he was probably very strong, which must have been important on the arduous journey to the Antipodes. Some would say a strong young man should be out of doors on such a pleasant day, riding or hunting or fishing. Instead, he spent much of his time here in the library decoding the mysteries of nature. I found him daunting, a man like no other I had ever met.

'I've put them in order of merit, with the best one on top,' I said, and tore away the tissue paper to reveal the passion flowers.

'What is it?'

'You know what it is, Flemynge. Don't say you can't tell what flower I have drawn.'

'What is its Latin name?'

'I have it here . . .' I scrabbled in my pocket, eventually bringing out a heavily creased piece of paper. '*Passiflora incarnata*.'

'Surely, you could have remembered just six Latin names, Elinor.'

'Yes, I suppose so. But what do you think of my painting? Have I not caught the mystical feeling of this plant, its religious associations?'

'The plant is not mystical and has no religious associations. Those stories were made up long after the Crucifixion. It isn't what I wanted,' he said and laid the painting aside to look at the next one.

I took it up and briskly put the passion flowers back on top of the stack. 'And why exactly isn't it what you wanted? That is a very good painting.'

'It's a muddle. I can't see what it is exactly. You certainly haven't done a botanical drawing. You preferred the religious associations, you say. If so, why have you been so careless? The story is that the various parts of the flower represent different facts about the Crucifixion. Very well then, where are the apostles? I can only see nine on the clearest bloom, and can't make them out at all on the others. And the five wounds of Christ? You've painted six. I expected to see some foliage in the picture. You haven't even painted the curling tendrils which are supposed to represent the lash of the persecutors.'

'It was just an impression,' I murmured wretchedly. 'The flowers are supposed to be weeping.'

Once again, he removed the passion flowers to look at the next painting. '*Rosa centifolia muscosa alba*,' I said through gritted teeth, and he smiled wryly as he quickly sorted through the remaining pictures until he came to the last.

'What's this?'

'Hume's Blush tea-scented China rose!' I shouted.

'I'm afraid you have made a shambles of this one. Why didn't you spend some time on it?'

'Spend some time? Why, I worked very hard on that ugly thing. I can't think why you wanted me to paint it. I could not find a single decent bloom on the plant.'

'I wanted you to paint it because it is a very important discovery. It doesn't matter that neither plant nor bloom is particularly attractive. Look at what should have been the high centre of the bloom. This bush came all the way from Canton in China just four years ago. Sir Anthony Hume received several at his home in Hertfordshire. I was amazed when I saw it in the conservatory. I rode over to Wormleybury this week, and Sir Anthony assured me that he had indeed given one bush to Presscott, who didn't appreciate it, of course. Yes, you really should have tried here, Elinor. Rose growers will breed new roses from this plant.'

I threw up my hands. 'Oh, in that case, I have been very stupid. I should have painted its sexual parts as well.'

'Yes, you should.' As I gaped at him, he opened one of the books to show me a botanical illustration. 'See, here, how Ferdinand Baur has painted the flower in its entirety in the centre of the page. He has put in every detail visible to the eye. And down here in the left-hand corner, he has bisected a bloom and painted its reproductive parts – stamens, styles, pollen. That is what I wanted you to do. And the name should have been written at the bottom of each picture.'

'That is an accurate record of a particular plant, I grant you. But the picture doesn't *speak*, Flemynge. It contains nothing of the artist, nothing of his emotions.'

'I told you I wanted a *record* of six plants. I distinctly remember using the word record. I didn't ask for your emotions, of which I get quite enough in real life.' He began to gather the paintings into a pile, his lips clamped tightly together. The angry schoolmaster.

I snatched the paintings from his hands and, with one gesture, tore them all in half and flung the pieces in the air. 'Do your own paintings in the future. I will not work for you.'

He turned, so tall and angry that I took a step backwards. 'Elinor, go to your room this instant and stay there until I come for you.'

'You can't mean what you're saying. I'm not a child who can be ordered to bed without its supper. You cannot mean to treat me in this way.'

'I had not meant to, no. But then, I had not expected you to lose all your self control so shamefully.'

After one still moment of disbelief, I ran from the

library and all the long way to my room. There I lay down on the bed and closed my eyes, trying to think what to do next.

The door opened and Millichip thudded into the room, the perfect picture of embarrassment.

I sat up. 'What do you want?'

'Master says I'm to close the shutters, ma'am. He said you wanted to rest in a darkened room.' The clumsy girl bounded about, banging shutters, then falling against furniture in the newly created gloom. She was gone within two minutes.

I lay back on the bed and closed my eyes again. But not for long; a single knock preceded Flemynge's entrance. He came over and sat down diffidently on the side of the bed. I sat up and began to place a few pillows at my back, shrugging off Flemynge's attempt to help.

'Are you fully recovered?' he asked. 'Rest in a darkened room can be very beneficial, I'm told.' I stared at him with hate. 'I want you to lead a calm, ordered existence, Elinor. I want you to learn to control your emotions and to think before you act.'

'As you do.'

'Yes,' he said carefully. 'I believe I do control my emotions and think things through before I act.'

'Did you think carefully before you married me, Flemynge?'

His laughter exploded in the room, shattering my hatred, as always, and unsettling me even further. 'No,' he said. 'I don't suppose I did. It was an impulsive act.'

'One you now bitterly regret.'

'Never, my dear, I assure you.'

He always spoke rapidly when lying, but I let it pass. 'Then there can be only one explanation for the way you treat me. You are trying to drive me mad.'

The smile vanished. The hard look which was Flemynge's defence against the world, settled into place on the sharp planes of his face. 'That is absurd. I don't believe you think that at all.'

'You wanted a wife whom everyone would think was mad. For what reason, I can't imagine. You have nothing to gain by it, except possibly pity. And I give you credit for not wanting pity from the people of Thorsby.'

He examined the scarred knuckles of one hand. 'You don't understand me at all.'

'We don't understand one another.'

Flemynge stood up. He looked tired and older than his years, and I wondered what thoughts lay behind that high forehead. 'I came to tell you that I must go to Chelmsford to talk to my lawyer . . . and to conduct some other business. I shall be gone all day.'

'May I leave this room?'

He shrugged. 'Do as you wish so long as you don't leave the grounds.'

I waited until I was sure he had left for Chelmsford, then gathered my painting equipment and went into the conservatory. The air was close, defying me to draw one calm breath, but I had to make haste. A storm was brewing and the light would soon deteriorate.

I settled the easel, chair and paint stand, pinned a fresh piece of paper to the board, then walked over to the Hume's Blush rose and held up one drooping head. The buds were singularly pointed. It was true: I had never seen a rose like it.

'Now then, you damned tea-scented rose, I'm going to look at you until you have no secrets from me, I'm going to paint you as you are, insipid and weakly, every vein of every petal. You can't escape me for I have a magnifying glass. And when I've finished painting you dressed in your tawdry finery. I shall take my knife and cut you in half from top to bottom so that I can paint you in the nude, like an anatomy lesson. How many artists murder their models, I wonder?'

# Chapter Six

I don't know what woke me that night. Certainly not the growl of thunder, which had, after all, been rattling round the edges of the horizon for hours as I sat waiting for Flemynge to return home. At eleven o'clock, I had gone upstairs to bed and by that time gusting winds were tearing at the windows. Nevertheless, I fell into a troubled sleep almost immediately. It must have been the fragment of some forgotten dream which caused me to come fully awake in an instant, feeling nerve-wracked and unable to lie still.

I left my bed and found my way to the door. Locked! I tried the handle several times, then felt the sharp edges of the keyhole, unable to believe the key was missing and that I had been locked in. When, finally, I admitted to myself that I was not going to be able to leave my room by this door, I felt an overwhelming sense of panic. When I had left my bed, it was with the idea of walking downstairs to the saloon merely for a change of surroundings. Now, I had to get out, felt compelled to escape.

Feeling my way along the wall, I soon came to the small hidden door that led to Millichip's room. This I found to be unlocked. Millichip slept in a room of a decent size, but the air was foul. I tiptoed the few feet necessary to reach her door to the hallway, knowing which way to go because a flash of lightning had momentarily illuminated the crack under the door. I was safely in the hall in seconds.

The stairs were easily negotiated because of the skylight. I went directly to the saloon and dragged open the shutters of the six ten-foot-tall windows as the thunder muttered churlishly far away.

I know that walking through the house without a candle at dead of night is a strange thing to do, but it is a habit of mine. I first began my night perambulations when I went to live with my aunt and uncle. It was not a very great adventure for a fourteen-year-old girl, but it gave me a great sense of freedom. My aunt watched me all the time, determined, as she put it, to make a proper young lady out of me. Her constant corrections – sit up straight, don't speak so loudly, mind your manners – were very oppressive to a young girl who had been brought up in a less strict household. But neither she nor my uncle ever found out about my night walks. Those times belonged to me.

On this night, I sat down on one of the settees, settling myself to watch the storm approach, but almost immediately the saloon door opened.

'Who's there?' said the man silhouetted in the doorway.

'It's only me, Flemynge,' I said. 'I didn't know you had returned home.'

'A broken wheel delayed me. What the devil are you doing down here? Why have you opened the shutters?'

'I wanted to watch the storm. The perfect place, don't you agree? It's coming towards us, and here I have a seat in the stalls. Why don't you join me?'

He shuffled forward, advancing cautiously, his booted feet ringing on the bare boards. 'Did you walk down here in the dark?'

'As you did.'

'I heard a noise and followed. I thought I was stalking a burglar, so I didn't want to take a candle. I do not regularly walk about in the dark, I assure you.'

'I do. I love the night. It hides all our imperfections and frees us from the necessity of maintaining civilized expressions. No need for false smiles in the dark.'

'A novel attitude.' He felt his way to the settee opposite me.

Rain struck the dozens of windowpanes with one concerted clash and streamed down the glass. Heavy black clouds were momentarily back-lit by lightning. The thunder was advancing inexorably, and drowned our low voices whenever it chose to speak.

'Isn't it wonderful?' I cried.

'You shouldn't be down here,' said Flemynge. 'Aren't you afraid of thunderstorms?'

'No, they relieve some of the tension in me.'

'Did you rest today, Elinor? You were very upset this morning.'

'No, or perhaps the correct answer is yes. I painted. That is a form of rest.'

'You should not have torn up your work. I was stupidly critical and have regretted it. All day the memory of your passion flowers has haunted me. It was strange, that painting. I've not seen one like it. Sort of, well, sort of like a wallpaper pattern.' He ignored my laughter. 'I wish you would paint them again.'

Lightning lit his face; the harsh lines gave an impression of strength, and perhaps of some deep sorrow.

It occurred to me that he was finding it hard to apologize for his actions. 'Your pictures disturbed me,' he said after a slight pause. 'I saw them as sloppy, undisciplined and unfettered, which is certainly not my view of the well-ordered plant kingdom. But that was no excuse for rudeness.'

Impulsively, I left my settee to sit on my heels before him. 'Do you know what I painted today? Hume's Blush tea-scented rose! You were right, Flemynge. I had failed to look at the rose carefully. My excuse must be that I am not a very good painter, but I shall improve. And I will paint some more passion flowers. Two sorts of paintings, you see. First with the eye of a naturalist, then with the eye of an artist.'

'I am very pleased,' he said gently. 'I would not blame you if you never wanted to paint a flower again.'

The storm was increasing its power, growing nearer. Lightning and thunder came almost simultaneously now.

'Oh, Flemynge, don't you feel the excitement of storms? They're wild and free. Please don't think it odd of me to come down here. In the dark, it's possible to forget that one is lonely. To tell you the truth, I feel restless. I want . . . but that's just it. I don't know what I want. The trouble is, I can't settle, can't be at peace with myself until I find it.'

He didn't speak, but reached out to caress my cheek, slipping his fingers in amongst the short curls. Instinctively, I bent my head to trap his hand between cheek and shoulder, hungry for his gentling touch.

A devastating bolt of lightning reached from the heavens and struck the huge oak tree in the garden. And with it came a clap of thunder that deafened me, setting my ears ringing as the old tree crashed to the ground.

'Oh, how tragic!' I cried and ran to the window, where it was impossible to see anything in the pitch dark through the torrents on the windowpanes. 'I shall miss that tree. All those years standing guard over Thorsby and now it's gone. How old do you suppose it was?'

'Two hundred years, perhaps more.' He joined me at the window, but I could tell by the coldness in his voice that he regretted our little moment of intimacy. 'I don't want you to roam this house in the dark. It is unwise.'

'Is that why you locked my door?'

'I thought you might be in the habit of sleep-walking. I –'

'Oh, you fool! What is the matter with you? Don't you know you can't lock me up? Has no one told you that lunatics are cunning? I had been planning to run away this morning. Instead, I stayed to paint Hume's Blush rose for *you*. There, you see? You have succeeded in your aim of driving me mad. Why else would I stay with you?'

I stumbled past him, heading for the door.

The next day began badly with the arrival of the remainder of the furniture I had ordered.

The dining table invited Flemynge's scorn. It was round and designed to seat ten persons, four of whom would have to contend with a leg, as he pointed out. But it was the centre-piece that drew his sneers. First of all, there was a circular section that turned, enabling those seated at the table to move the dishes round and serve themselves. This was quite a novel idea, I thought. Unfortunately, there rose from this tray a three-tiered dumb waiter, each level slightly smaller than the one below it, the whole towering some three feet above the table. If we sat on opposite sides of this monstrosity, said Flemynge, we would not be able to see one another at all.

Fortunately, he used up most of his sarcasm on the table, so that he had comparatively little to say about the sideboard, the chairs and the half dozen little tables – all in the Egyptian style – with which I proposed to fill the family rooms. However, he told me exactly what he thought of my taste when the Polonaise bed for my chamber had been assembled. By that time, he had learned the cost of all this furniture, which further fuelled his anger. I didn't feel I could whole-heartedly defend my ill-considered choices, and was near to tears by the time he announced that he was riding out with Mr Stornaway on estate business.

I had no more desire than he did to sit in either the morning-room or the drawing-room, and even less intention of spending this glorious day in my chamber with the Polonaise bed. So, as usual, I took refuge out of doors with my paints. Needless to say, my disquiet led to a lack of concentration which ensured that I would be dissatisfied with my work.

As the day wore on, it grew oppressively hot, so I retreated indoors for a light luncheon before settling in the saloon with a book. The afternoon sun poured in through the tall windows, forcing me to pull the blinds, which cut out the sight of the stricken tree, even though I could still hear the drone of half a dozen saws at work.

I was wearing my flimsiest gown and Grecian sandals on my bare feet, but the heat still made me too drowsy to read. I was almost asleep when Flemynge walked in through the terrace doors, having been supervising the removal of the oak tree.

He, too, was dressed informally, the way I preferred to see him: riding breeches and boots, a white shirt open at the neck and his sleeves rolled up to reveal his muscular arms. He must have been riding bare-headed because the sun had reddened his forehead and the bridge of his nose a little. He looked the picture of animal health, and I saw with relief that he was no longer angry.

I cut off his first words of apology with a profuse apology of my own, and we were very soon laughing about the furniture, wondering what could be done with the table and concocting absurd ideas for furnishing the upper tiers. This promising and amusing discussion was interrupted by Grimsby carrying a card on a silver tray.

'Captain Thaddeus Dawnay,' read Flemynge aloud, and I saw at once that the name was not unfamiliar to him, nor was he surprised at Tad's coming to call. He must have seen my letter and actually read it before allowing it to be sent.

'Bring the gentleman in here, Grimsby,' said Flemynge, and then sarcastically to me: 'What a pity you aren't dressed in some of your finery, Elinor.'

There was no time to answer before Tad swaggered into the room, just as surprised as the Maltbys had been by the eccentric decoration.

We must have made a strange-looking trio: Flemynge and I improperly dressed to receive visitors; Tad wearing very high, starched shirt-points, a blue tailcoat and narrow black knitted pantaloons which ended above his ankles. I had forgotten how handsome a man he was.

I had forgotten also that he was a good deal older than I, thirty-seven or -eight. Today he looked every one of his years with an uncertain smile rapidly fading from his tanned face.

'Come in, Captain Dawnay,' said Flemynge.

'Mr Flemynge! I am in your debt, sir, for taking my dear betrothed from that despicable place. I would have rescued her myself if I had known where she was.'

'You didn't learn that my wife was in that *despicable place* from her letter, Captain. So, I wonder, how did you find out that she was in Chennings?'

I looked away when I saw a high flush flare in Tad's cheeks, then turned back again to ask: 'Did you know what my uncle proposed to do to me, Tad? Did you know where I was?'

'*Your wife?*' exclaimed Tad, not attending to me at all.

'You did know, didn't you, Tad?' I said more loudly.

'Answer my wife's question, Captain Dawnay,' said Flemynge. 'She is entitled to an explanation.'

'Well, sir, I –'

'In fact, you informed Mr Burns-Roberts where he might find his niece. Come now, Captain. I know the whole story. My lawyer has visited the Royal Oak and spoken to the landlord's wife. Did she not tell you so? Elinor arrived at the Royal Oak looking for you last January. You made her share a chamber with Mrs Dedworthy. Two days later, her uncle arrived saying his niece was insane and he was proposing to have her committed to Chennings. No one but you knew where Elinor's uncle lived. Everyone would have been eager to tell you what happened to Elinor the minute you returned from wherever you had hidden yourself that day. Why did you do it? Was it because there was no chance of your getting your hands on her money?'

I said: 'Oh, Tad!' and sat down again.

'I think you have no idea of her suffering during the months she spent in that madhouse. You couldn't even spare the time to drive a few miles to visit her, could you?' said Flemynge.

Tad bowed stiffly. 'Since Elinor is married, I have no business to be here, Mr Flemynge. I came here today only because she asked me to —'

'— take her away. Yes, I know. It is not too late. The marriage hasn't been consummated. I'm sure an annulment could be obtained on the grounds that I abducted her from Chennings and forced her into marriage. I won't deny it.'

At that moment, I hated them both. Neither of them wanted me; each was politely declining to be my husband. Or no, Tad was considering my worth, and possibly wondering if I were my aunt's heiress.

'I feel bound to inform you,' continued Flemynge in a conversational tone, 'that Elinor's uncle stole her entire fortune and disposed of the estate, due to a pressing need to avoid being arrested. I have written to her aunt, but the letter was returned. Apparently, Mrs Burns-Roberts has gone away. However, Elinor's lack of fortune will not weigh with *you*, Captain, since I can see you are deeply in love with my wife.'

Tad's brown hair was flecked with grey; there were deep lines at the corners of his blue eyes and down each side of his mouth. His sort of handsomeness depended almost entirely on a charming manner and debonair smile. Standing now, nervously fingering the brim of his hat, he looked a sorry figure, entirely lacking Flemynge's powerful air.

'I am penniless, Tad,' I said. 'I don't know what possessed me to write to you. I'm really much better off staying with my rich husband. Besides, he lied to you. We have spent many passionate nights together.'

From the corner of my eye, I saw Flemynge smile briefly. 'Well said, my dear,' he murmured. 'You *will* be better off as my wife. I cannot picture you leading a hand-to-mouth existence as a smuggler's woman. The

Captain, you know, lives by frequent journeys across the Channel under cover of darkness. On the other hand, I have no wish to stand in the way of true love.'

While Tad was trying to think of something to say, I turned to Flemynge. 'On the other hand, *dear* Flemynge, if I leave, you will be free to marry the magnificent Miss Makin.'

Flemynge smiled broadly. 'Miss Makin is married. I, therefore, have no objections to keeping you.'

Still Tad was silent. 'You may go now,' I said bitterly. 'I apologize for bringing you all this way, but I am afraid you are too poor for me. I've a mind to lead the grand life. Already, my husband and I have been invited to a fashionable ball. I shall wear the Flemynge diamond and emerald parure.'

'I wish you well,' said Tad, 'and must take your word for it that you will be leading a grand life, in spite of the fact that you appear to have married a navvy!'

So saying, he turned and strode out through the door. Flemynge shouted after him: 'I'm in the market for several casks of French brandy next time you visit the Continent!'

There was no reply. Flemynge and I regarded one another coldly. 'How do you know my estate has been disposed of?' I asked.

'I don't. I do know that your uncle embezzled some money, but managed to pay it all back to the rightful owners before a seizure carried him away. That is common knowledge among City men.'

'Why didn't you tell me about this before? How long have you known?'

'Dear wife, I was waiting until your swain put in an appearance. You did not suppose I would put myself out to find your fortune for *him*, did you?'

'You are a horrible cold-hearted man. I wish I still owned the Old Manor House. I wished I lived there instead of in this hateful place.'

'Quite,' he said. 'A way must be found to restore your rightful possessions to you. I propose going to London and will leave within the hour. I promise you I will track your aunt to the ends of the earth if need be.'

'Thank you, but there are a good many things I want to say to you.'

'We will talk at length when I return. For now, please excuse me.' He bowed formally as if to a complete stranger and left the room.

It was with the greatest reluctance that I retired to my Polonaise bed that night, although the style of it no longer seemed strange, much less ugly. After all, my chamber was very large and the ceiling was extremely high. A bed with a central crown-shaped canopy twelve feet above the ground with gilding, a two-foot-wide fringed drape around it and great swags of fringed gold silk looping down to the bedposts and on to the floor level might look ludicrous in a smaller room. In this one, the bulk and excessive decoration merely helped to fill the space.

Flemynge was wrong about my bed and a great deal else, I thought, as I went up the short pair of steps to slide between the sheets. I was exhausted from a day spent reliving the disturbing encounter with Tad and even more disturbing discussion with Flemynge. I was determined to say a great many strong things to my husband when he returned, and these I rehearsed all day. Now I was desperate for sleep, for an escape from my thoughts. And so, naturally, I could not sleep at all.

After five or ten minutes spent tossing about, I threw back the covers and swung my legs over the side of the bed, intending to fold back my shutters and open a window. Unfortunately, I forgot about the little set of steps and tumbled from bed to floor, cracking a shin on the steps as I fell on to my hands and knees. Now very angry, but with no one to blame for my fall except myself, I stumbled over to the window, folded back the shutters with a crash and threw up one of the sash windows in order to lean out.

The air was still, as damp and almost as warm out of doors as in my room, but my shin had ceased to throb quite so painfully, the moon was full and the garden looked enchanting bathed in its ghostly light. I began to feel a little more cheerful.

The gardeners had left very little of the old oak. How I would miss it! There was nothing left now but a stump fully two yards across and two feet high. Flemynge had spoken of the need to plant another tree when the old stump had been completely removed, but the new tree's shade would not be of use to me for many summers to come. In the meantime, I would have to look elsewhere for a protected place to sit.

The terrace below me looked very inviting at this time of night, but on a bright day the hot sun warmed the flagstones until they were unbearable even through the soles of my sandals. I scanned the length of the terrace, wondering how one might give shade to a small portion. It was not until I looked directly downwards that I noticed the doors from the terrace to the saloon were standing slightly ajar.

Locking up at night was Grimsby's responsibility. I would have a word with him in the morning. In the meantime, I must go downstairs, because I could not allow the doors to stand open for the rest of the night. Without bothering to light a candle or to put on a robe and slippers, I let myself out of my room by the proper door thanking heaven that Flemynge had not instructed Mrs Hobson to lock me in my room while he was away.

Downstairs, I soon realized that not only were the saloon doors open, but several of the shutters were folded back. Since my eyes were perfectly accustomed to the dark, I could see reasonably well – well enough, at least to know that I was alone in the room. No crouching figure near the furniture would leap out at me as I passed.

The shutters were very heavy; I started on the left side of the room and was a little out of breath from the exertion by the time I reached the central pair of doors. I was just about to pull the doors together and lock them, when I heard a noise away over to my right. I turned to look in the direction of the sound, but there was nothing to see. Perhaps mice, I thought, and turned speedily back to my work. I disliked mice.

The shutters were not important. I would simply lock the doors and go back to my bed, which suddenly seemed very inviting.

A slight creaking from the dark corner raised goose flesh all over me and made my scalp tingle. I looked round almost involuntarily in time to see a white-gowned wraith materialize out of nowhere. I could not move and certainly could not speak. I had no choice but to stand where I was and await events.

Fortunately for my sanity, I remembered that this room also had a cunningly disguised door set flush with the wall in that dark corner. I knew then that the wraith was a woman, flesh and blood, after all. Like me, she was in bare feet and wore a nightgown. Like me she had no nightcap; like mine, her hair was short. Showing no sign of surprise or hesitation, she walked towards me, and was less than ten feet away when I recognized her as the frail sister of Aubrey Presscott. Anger rescued me from paralysis.

'What on earth are you doing here?'

'You killed the oak tree,' she said, her tone of voice perfectly calm as if her being in the saloon at this hour were the most natural thing in the world.

With trembling fingers, I managed to unlock the doors and push them wide. 'Get out, Miss Presscott. You have no right to be here.'

'You will be punished for killing the tree.'

'What a ridiculous thing to say! You must be –' And although I didn't say it, I knew instinctively that she *was* mad. I had seen that dreamy withdrawn expression before, heard a woman speak utter nonsense in the voice of sweet reason. I knew more about madness than most people, and I was in no doubt about Miss Presscott.

'I will come again and punish you. You are a wicked witch.' On those words, she walked calmly through the open doors, across the terrace and on to the lawn. I watched until she was lost in deep shadow, then locked the doors and ran upstairs to my bed. It was some time before I slept.

My interview the next day with Grimsby was far from satisfactory. He had *not* left the shutters open, nor the doors unlocked. Surely, I was mistaken. About Miss Lucinda Presscott, he really couldn't comment. The Presscotts' butler, Barlow, had followed the family to Essex Grange, while Mrs Hobson had chosen to stay at Thorsby. Grimsby had been taken on by Mr Flemynge and had never even seen Miss Presscott. Nevertheless, he doubted – and left unsaid exactly what it was he doubted.

Mrs Hobson was not so careful in her choice of words. She sought me out in the morning-room before I had finished my second cup of coffee. I must have dreamed the whole thing, she said. It was not possible. She had worked for the Presscott family for ten years and, had, therefore, known the Presscott girl since childhood. Miss Lucinda would not come to Thorsby in her nightgown. Why, Thorsby was all of two miles from Essex Grange! Someone would have seen her on the way.

I saw where the discussion was leading. I knew I must not give the servants further cause to doubt my sanity, so I agreed with Mrs Hobson, dragging my expression into a light-hearted smile as I did so. Of course! That was the explanation! I had been dreaming!

Mrs Hobson was not finished with me, however. Surely, I had walked in my sleep? Mrs Hobson only mentioned it because some of the shutters *had* been found open this morning. Since the person who opened them could not possibly be a young woman who lived two miles away, why then, they must have been opened by me. If I had not consciously done it, then I must have been walking in my sleep. Did I not agree?

I was left with no alternative but to say yes, I had probably walked in my sleep, opened the shutters and dreamt that Miss Lucinda Presscott had come to call in her nightgown.

Thereafter, I kept to myself, speaking to no one unless it was absolutely necessary, not even to the gossipy dressmaker who came to discuss my gown for the Maltby party. On the third day, I ran out of paints. Mr Stornaway was perfectly willing to ride into Chelmsford to purchase supplies for me. He absolutely refused to buy me any more novels, however. Mr Flemynge had spoken to him on the subject. I did understand didn't I? I nodded and left his cramped office before he had a chance to see my tears.

On the sixth day, just as the sun was setting, Flemynge returned, walking through the French doors into the saloon where I had been sitting for some time. After the briefest of greetings, he announced that he had found my aunt and persuaded her to give him the name of the new owner of my estate. He had then travelled on to Gloucestershire. Unfortunately, the new owner refused to sell, but Flemynge was not discouraged. He was sure that if he offered the right price, he could buy the Old Manor House eventually, and when it came into his hands, I could go there to live on a generous allowance. Without waiting for my reaction to this outrageous suggestion, he said he was very tired and intended to go to bed immediately.

I was given no chance to say anything at all. Throughout the entire interview, I had not even moved, and by the time he left the room, I felt too weak to stand up. I suppose I must have stayed on in the saloon for half an hour or more, sensing total defeat, yet knowing I must continue to fight for my security.

It was necessary, I decided, to try to see events through Flemynge's eyes if I were to understand his behaviour. In the first place, he knew I had written to Tad, asking him to take me away. It had been a mistake to deceive Flemynge, to tell him I had no one to turn to that day he took me away from Chennings. I had given him reason to think me sly.

Then I had mistakenly allowed him to visit my aunt. Yet how could I have prevented him? Aunt Burns-Roberts hated me; I could imagine the sort of tales she would have delighted in telling. I must assume Flemynge thought he had good reason for wanting to send me away.

I, on the other hand, had every reason to want to stay, to be a true wife to him. The prospect of living at the Old Manor House without him appalled me. I would be shunned, a married woman who had mislaid her husband! Or worse! What if he tired of waiting to buy my estate? Might he not simply send me out into the world? I would starve! Scenes of desperation filled my mind. It mustn't happen. A woman situated as I would be, would have no hope of staying alive except by prostitution. Something had to be done to secure my position as Flemynge's legal wife.

By the time Grimbsy let himself into the saloon, affecting surprise that I was still there, I had made my plans, and coolly told him to lock up securely before I went upstairs to my room. What I proposed to do set my cheeks on fire and caused me to feel a trifle weak-kneed, but I told myself these were desperate times. I must be courageous.

So, courageously, I put on my prettiest nightgown, brushed my short hair until it gleamed and sprayed myself liberally with scent. Then, courageously, I blew out my candle and started towards the door.

Millichip's little door opened. 'Did you want me to help you undress, ma'am?' asked the maid.

'No thank you. As you see, I'm already undressed, have put out the light and plan to get into bed. You are a little late with your offer of help.'

'Oh, ma'am, don't say that!' The girl was fairly hopeless as a lady's maid, but now and then her conscience disturbed her; she knew she led an idle life, the envy of the entire staff. On these occasions, I was forced to endure her clumsy attentions for a few minutes until she convinced herself that she was indeed earning her keep, after which I might be comfortable again.

On this night, she picked up her candle, clucking like a mother hen, and came to my chamber to help me into bed, to smooth the covers and ask several times over if there was anything I required.

When she had returned to her own quarters, I lay blinking at the darkness. I don't know how long I waited, but it seemed like hours, until I felt sure that Millichip was asleep. My spirit almost failed me; I had been given too much time to consider the wisdom of my plan.

Somehow, I found the strength of mind to rise from the bed, to leave my room, and to walk very quietly into Flemynge's. It was as dark as my own, and I didn't know its furnishings or their positions at all well, having been in the room only once or twice.

Eventually, I found the bed; Flemynge seemed to be lying on the far side, facing away from me. With the greatest possible stealth, and shaking like the proverbial leaf, I slid into bed beside him and lay on my back. I could hear his steady breathing, could feel the heat of his body close to mine. And had not the slightest idea what to do next.

How did one seduce one's husband? What, *exactly*, was involved? And what an absolutely idiotic thing for me to have done in coming here! I supposed I might stay all night and greet him in friendly fashion in the morning. Or I might now tap him on the shoulder and . . . what?

I had been a fool, committed an act of folly greater than anything I had ever done in my uncle's house. What a figure of fun I must look! The whole situation was ridiculous. I would have to return to my room before Flemynge woke and pray he never found out what a fool I had been.

Unfortunately, the knowledge that I must not make the slightest movement to awaken him, brought on a perverse, hysterical desire to giggle like a schoolgirl. I bit my knuckles, shaking with silent laughter, squeezing my eyelids together as tears rolled down my temples on to the pillow. The more I tried to control my emotions, the more I wanted to laugh, nervous laughter, the high-pitched irrational sort that one always finds so irritating in others.

'What the devil do you think you're doing?' asked Flemynge suddenly.

I swear the sound of his voice stopped my heart for several seconds. I no longer felt the urge to giggle, or laugh or even smile.

'Well –'

'Well?' he said, helpfully.

'I can't explain.'

'Were you walking in your sleep?'

'Yes, that's it,' I said with relief. 'Or no! Most definitely not! They will tell you that I walk in my sleep, but I don't.'

'Who will tell me?'

'The servants.'

'Elinor –' He moved towards me, or at least I thought he did.

Like a frightened animal, I scrambled to the very edge

of the bed. 'I made a mistake, Flemynge. I should not be here.'

'You meant to get into your own bed, is that it?'

'Exactly.' I was up and moving towards the door. 'Good night. We must talk in the morning. I don't know what my aunt may have told you about me, but –'

'Nothing that prepared me for this night's business,' he said in a voice of deep disgust.

Burning with shame, I returned to my room.

Birdsong woke me, a determined chirruping that I couldn't shut out of my dreams. The windows were wide open, the day promised rain, and I was cold. Desperately, I pulled the covers over my head, but it was no use. Flemynge would be in the morning-room taking his breakfast, and I was going to have to face him some time. Besides, Millichip was thumping round the room like an elephant; her simple good humour would soon grate, convincing me I would prefer my husband's coldness to the maid's simple-minded chatter.

When I entered the morning-room a quarter of an hour later, there was an empty egg-stained plate in front of Flemynge. We glared at one another as he flung his napkin on the table.

When he made to leave the room, I put out a hand to stop him. 'You can't walk out of the room the instant I enter it. I won't allow you to run away.'

'I have nothing to say to you.' He brushed me aside, but I followed him out of the room.

With long strides, he left the house by a back door, crossed the flagged terrace and leapt down the four broad steps on to the lawn which was still silvered with dew.

'Come back here, you coward!' I ran down the sloping lawn and caught up with him finally on the stone bridge. He was leaning over the wall, gazing into the dull stream; I was too breathless to speak.

'In case you were wondering,' said Flemynge, 'your aunt never mentioned a tendency to climb into the beds of strange men.'

'I never! And, what's more, you aren't –'

'She *did* say you climbed out of your bedroom window and walked with your maid to a low inn. I should have guessed that much. How else were you to meet a rogue like Dawnay? I suppose you think I was flattered by your arrival last night. You are mistaken. I assume I am the last in a long line.'

'Well, you *are* a strange man,' I said. 'Very strange. You are also my husband and the first man I have ever been so near. I don't expect you to believe me, but it's true. In my youth I *may* have been rather more daring than other girls –'

'A masterly understatement.'

'But never as wild as the meekest boy.'

'There is a difference.'

'Oh, I know there is a difference. There is also a difference between young ladies who have never been sent to madhouses and those who have. My experiences have set me apart for all time. I am different, I admit, but surely you can see –'

'I was an old man by the time I reached the advanced age of ten, ushering in my mother's lovers. I, who had no real family, was given a succession of "uncles" who stayed for weeks or months and then disappeared for ever. I vowed I would never marry a woman like my mother. Can you imagine my emotions when I awoke to find you beside me last night?'

'Of course, I understand,' I said. 'Do *you* understand that I am not in the least like her? I'm not, I tell you.'

'Mama wanted security and money from her gentlemen friends. Can you honestly say that those considerations did not weigh with you last night? Were you not simply trying to ensure that I could never get rid of you? Well, let me put your mind at rest. I will always acknowledge you as my wife; you will never be short of funds. There now. You need not make the grand sacrifice, after all.'

It began to rain, huge drops that struck at an angle, born on a fresh wind. Flemynge walked away in the direction of the stables, leaving me with no choice but to return to the house. I thought I had reached the lowest point in my marriage, but my husband searched me out that evening to push me further down. Clearly, he had been discussing me with the servants.

'Elinor, I have come to tell you that I believe, as does Mrs Hobson, that the Presscott girl could not possibly have been here.' He was speaking in his other voice, the fatherly one full of concern for my mental health. I preferred him angry, because then he treated me as if I were a normal irritating woman.

'I know it sounds unlikely,' I answered patiently, 'but I assure you, the girl is unbalanced. Don't you think I know by this time what a lunatic looks like, how one acts? Please believe me. I can't bear it if you also think I'm mad.'

He sat down beside me on the sphinx-head settee and asked me to describe carefully how I happened to leave my room and go to the saloon, what I had been doing when I first saw Miss Presscott. When I had repeated every detail to him, he said: 'And now tell me exactly what the girl was wearing.'

'A nightgown, bare feet and no cap.'

'And you?'

I sighed. 'The same.'

He was all sympathy and understanding: 'A very unnerving sensation, seeing a strange woman in the saloon. It must have upset you deeply.' I agreed wholeheartedly. Then he spoiled everything by saying: 'I expect Grimsby is lying. It must have been he who left the shutters open. Try to put the incident entirely out of your mind. You suffered horrendous shocks during your stay at Chennings. It is no wonder that you occasionally have . . . It's growing late. Had you not better dress for the Maltby's party?'

I had forgotten about the party, and was really not in the mood for an evening of gaiety and meeting new people, but I nodded dumbly and left the room.

# Chapter Seven

Flemynge looked magnificent in his evening wear. He also looked impatient, and pointedly consulted his watch as I entered the family drawing-room.

'Flemynge, do you like it?'

'Like what?'

'My gown, of course! I had the over-tunic and the turban made of emerald green to complement the jewels. But now I think the ensemble makes me look thirty years old.'

He smiled. 'At least.'

'This is not a joking matter. Shall I remove the over-tunic and just wear the white satin gown? And what about the turban? Perhaps just some flowers or a feather in my hair?'

'You look very elegant as you are, and there is not enough time to change your mind or your gown. We are going to be the last to arrive as it is.'

I tugged on the ends of my gloves, flexing my fingers nervously. 'You don't understand. My appearance is important. I don't want to give anyone an excuse to criticize me.'

'How can you suppose that what you wear will affect the gossips? If you wear a turban, they will say you shouldn't. If you wear flowers, they will say you should have worn a turban. I fail to understand why women find these things so important.'

I allowed him to take my arm and pull me along towards the carriage. 'I've been to balls before, you know. Extravagant balls where every woman was wearing expensive jewels and fine gowns.'

'Then you have more experience than I,' he said. 'In

the past, I attended a few public assemblies and found them incredibly dull. I never expected to be invited to a ball given by a baronet.'

After that, neither of us spoke on the short drive to Albany House. The Maltby's home was less than half the size of Thorsby and the receiving rooms were low-ceilinged, panelled in oak and, at the moment, uncomfortably crowded.

Sir Hesketh and Lady Maltby had greeted us warmly enough when our turn came to shake their hands in the receiving line, but as we walked into the drawing-room, I didn't see a familiar face until Clarissa Maltby came up to us rather shyly and stammered out a welcome.

I was excessively grateful to her and began to talk rapidly in order to hide my nervousness. Then some red-faced gentleman hailed Flemynge and he left my side before I had finished gabbling about what a warm night it was and how we had enjoyed quite a succession of them recently.

'To whom is my husband speaking?' I asked Clarissa when I had run out of things to say about the weather.

'Colonel Sotherby. I expect your husband knows him because they are both magistrates.'

I had heard Flemynge mention the colonel and felt that the latter should have called on us, but there was no time to consider this piece of rudeness, because Clarissa showed signs of wishing to leave my side. I found it necessary to hold her to me with a series of stupid questions until, after a few minutes, her eyes opened wide and her cheeks paled. I noticed that she was not looking at me but over my shoulder; I turned to see Mr Aubrey Presscott approaching.

'Oh, Aubrey –' began Clarissa uncertainly.

'So, Mrs Flemynge, we meet again,' said Mr Presscott, his girlish lips drawn back in an unpleasant smile. 'I must confess myself surprised to see you here. Clarissa, why . . . What a silly girl. She has fled, but she needn't have done so. We will not come to blows, will we? You look entrancing, Mrs Flemynge. Who would guess that just a few short weeks ago . . . but let us not speak of that. Yes, my dear, you are a rare beauty, in spite of no, I say *because* of those dainty freckles on your nose and cheeks. Let those who dislike such small marks of earthy beauty look elsewhere for their ideals.'

Clarissa had, indeed, melted away the instant Mr Presscott spoke to me, so I had no hesitation in replying to the odious man in the style he deserved. 'What a foppish oaf you are, sir! I find everything about you repulsive. Are you not afraid you will stab your cheek with your shirt points? By the way, tell your sister to stay away from Thorsby. I may be a wicked witch as she says I am. Then, who knows what evil deed I might commit?'

The smile never left the man's face, although he lowered his voice to reply in kind. 'Evil deeds have already been done. Thorsby should have been mine one day. Your husband stole it from my father. You will both be sorry, I promise you. I don't know what purpose the Maltby's had in inviting our family, a noble one well loved in the county, on the same evening as they have invited you and Flemynge. Unless . . . Yes, that's it! You and your husband are to be the entertainment. I expect later on you will both perform some tricks of sleight-of-hand. Relieving others of their property is your husband's special talent, isn't it?'

Before I could think of a suitable answer, he left me. I lifted my chin, now thoroughly angry, and went in search of better company. These people, grinning behind their fans and chatting about me, might think themselves greatly superior to City folks like my parents, but I thought they were merely badly dressed country bumpkins. I smiled invitingly at the first callow youth I caught staring openly at me, and did not lack company of a sort for the next two hours.

The women showed no such friendliness, however.

Not one of them spoke to me. They even looked away when I approached, fanning themselves furiously for fear I might actually speak to them directly.

Seated by one of the windows, Mrs Presscott, looking hot in tight lacings and puce satin, held court, her daughter sitting unsmilingly beside her. I was curious to see Lucinda Presscott in a well-lit room. She wore a low-cut cream silk gown and spoke to no one, while her mother never closed her mouth. No gentleman asked her to dance, none of the young girls came near her. I saw that her dark hair was not short after all; she wore it in a bun at the back with a wispy fringe covering her high forehead.

She and Clarissa Maltby were close to the same age and must have known each other all their lives, yet did not seem to be friends. Perhaps relations this evening were a little strained since their gowns were too similar to give either girl much pleasure.

While Miss Presscott was sullen, Clarissa looked sweet and vulnerable. Her hair would not stay in place, requiring constant adjustment; the flounce at the hem of her gown was beginning to come adrift and her gloves were already stained. Yet her ramshackle appearance seemed to bring out the protective instinct in the young men. She was never without a partner for a dance, an arm to lean on or someone to fetch her a lemonade.

Flemynge claimed me for supper.

'I compliment you on your success with the gentlemen,' he said. I chose to take the remark as a criticism.

There was a rather uncivilized dash for the supper tables and we quickly found ourselves in the middle of a crush. It was then that I heard a man's voice saying something about 'the prettiest mistress of Thorsby for generations'. I looked up at Flemynge to see if he had heard, and he winked at me.

'Yes,' said Lady Maltby in her piercing voice. 'I had hoped she would behave in an eccentric way, but apart from flirting with every man present, she has done nothing amusing at all.'

Flemynge bent his head to whisper: 'Eavesdropping is, after all, a lottery. One can never be sure if it is worth the effort. Just remember; Lady Maltby is a wit, and wit of her sort requires a victim. I must admit, I had expected to fill that particular role.'

I was too angry to say anything, and no longer hungry which was just as well because the food was overdressed and insufficient for such a crowd. To top it all, the wine was warm. That did not stop me from having three glasses, and I would have had a fourth except that Flemynge took the glass from my hand so that the footman couldn't fill it again.

For several minutes I gave serious thought to what I might do to create a sensation. I suppose it was fortunate that nothing occurred to me. I was beginning to feel rather tired. So many people, so much noise and chatter after months spent incarcerated in Chennings had exhausted me. I made my way into the drawing-room where a sprinkling of people were eating and talking in intimate groups. The rooms had grown unbearably hot and someone had boldly opened one of the French doors behind the closed curtains; I could feel a gentle breeze about my ankles.

Seeing that no one was looking in my direction, I slipped through the curtains and out on to the Maltby's narrow terrace. The long summer day had ended at last; the night was clear and the sky star-filled, but the moon was on the wane. In the enveloping darkness, I was just able to see Lucinda Presscott running down the path towards the gloom of the shrubbery.

Here was my chance to prove that I was right about the girl! I set my plate and fork down on the flagstones and ran after her, but she was out of sight before I had crossed the lawn. My only hope now of discovering what she was up to was to move in among the shrubs that lay on either side of the gravel path, because she would otherwise hear my footsteps.

The undergrowth was treacherous with tough branches and exposed roots, while the necessity to be silent as I moved, slowed my progress even further. I only discovered how near I was to her, when she hissed: 'Aubrey!'

So brother and sister were up to something! I hoped I would be able to hear what they said from my present position, because I could not move much closer.

With great daring, I inched my way carefully towards the path for a clearer view. Dark as it was, I could see their forms well enough to know that they were locked in an embrace, kissing noisily with sighs and moans that shocked me for an instant. Then common sense came to the rescue. Aubrey Presscott was not kissing his sister but Clarissa Maltby.

'Oh, Aubrey, if only we could marry,' she said at last, and I wondered how she had the breath to speak at all.

'Well, it's impossible, so we mustn't think of it. Your father is wise to forbid us, I suppose. I certainly must marry a wealthy woman. My father is dangerously ill, my dear, and not expected to live much longer. How ironic it all is! Had he died before Flemynge made his claim, I would have had possession of Thorsby and refused to move out. The lawyers would have been fighting over the house for years while I continued in residence. As it is, Father threw away the prize and I am reduced to penury. What possessed your parents to invite that bastard and his mad wife tonight, by the way?'

'Oh, Aubrey, I don't wish to hurt you, but . . . but they wish to be on good terms with whoever lives at Thorsby, and they do think Mr Flemynge is the rightful owner. Of course, *your* parents are their dearest friends and —'

'Yes, your parents are fond of being *dear* friends, yet

don't know the meaning of loyalty. I thank God my father was too ill to come here tonight. The sight of that lunatic throwing out lures to every man in the room would have killed him.'

'She *is* very beautiful. I didn't actually see her doing anything incorrect. Did you?'

Aubrey Presscott seemed not to be listening. 'Flemynge ruined us. I hope you know that. We are destitute.'

'But how can that be? You can't mean *destitute*, Aubrey. Your father is a partner in the Presscott and Stracey bank!'

'Which may have to close. There have been some irregularities. I believe your father suspects as much, which is partly why he has forbidden us to meet. Your parents, my dear Clarissa, are toad-eating, fortune-hunting –'

'Aubrey, stop that! I won't listen to another word. Besides, I must go back to the house. They must not discover that I met you out here in the dark and alone. I am so afraid of Mama. You don't know what cruel things she can say.'

There were a few more noisy kisses, several heartfelt sighs and then the lovers parted, Aubrey Presscott announcing that he intended to go for a long walk. He would not be returning to the party, but would call on Lady Maltby the next day. Within seconds, I could no longer hear the footsteps of either as they went in opposite directions.

Clarissa was not the only one who had been away from the party for too long. I must hurry back before I was missed. It was when I made the first move to leave the shrubbery that I discovered my white satin slippers had sunk an inch or two into the newly-forked earth. When I bent my head to feel what sort of state my slippers were in, the feather in my turban caught on a branch and broke off, while the turban itself was wrenched from my head.

And someone was approaching! Desperately, I pulled first one foot and then the other from the mud, lost my balance, and staggered out on to the path.

'Elinor, is that you?' said Flemynge. 'I have been looking everywhere for you. What the devil are you doing out here?'

'Well. I followed Lucinda Presscott because I thought she might be intending to go to Thorsby again. You see, I wanted to prove to you that I'm not –'

'Miss Presscott has not left her mother's side all evening. A strange young woman, I grant you, but she seems to have no intention of going anywhere. I met Miss Maltby on the path a moment ago. She said she had not seen you.'

'No, she didn't. I discovered that it was Clarissa whom I was following when she kept an assignation with Mr Aubrey Presscott and began kissing him! Just over there, they were. I heard everything they said.'

'A peeping Thomasina. Really, Elinor!'

'The Maltbys believe you are the proper owner of Thorsby and they refuse to let Aubrey court Clarissa. And, oh yes, the Presscott bank is in difficulties, so the Presscotts have no money and –'

'Have you not spied enough? Let us go back to the house.'

'But, Flemynge, I didn't mean to spy. It just happened. I couldn't very well tell them I was watching. Besides, I'm only telling you this because that man hates you. You must be careful.'

'I'm trembling with fright. Come along.'

I clutched his sleeve. 'Not just yet. I have lost most of the feather from my turban and my slippers are covered in mud.'

It was too dark to read his expression, but I heard him click his tongue in annoyance. 'There is an ornamental fishpond not too far from here. I will wet my handkerchief in the water and see if I can clean up your shoes. As for your turban, the only thing you can do is to remove the remnants of the feather.'

We spent the next ten minutes in almost total darkness trying to wash the mud off my slippers and put my turban in some sort of order. By the time we slipped through the curtains to rejoin the other guests, my feet were soaking wet and I had discovered a small but prominent tear in my over-tunic. No one, however, was at all interested in our appearance.

Seated on a settee, Mrs Presscott was in strong hysterics, wailing and calling for her dear Aubrey, while Lucinda, next to her mother, had her hands over her face as she rocked and sobbed loudly. The entire company seemed to be in a state of shock.

'What has happened?' asked Flemynge of the man nearest to him.

'Word has just come that Hildebrand Presscott is dead. Broke his heart over Thorsby, I imagine,' said the gentleman coldly.

Now, all eyes turned in our direction.

'*Murderer!*' screamed Mrs Presscott. Lucinda looked up at us and her fingers curled into claws. Someone placed a hand on her shoulder to prevent her from rising.

'I am sincerely sorry to hear of Mr Presscott's death,' said Flemynge. 'I do not feel myself to be responsible, however. Please excuse us. My wife is not feeling well, and I'm sure Mrs Presscott doesn't want us near her at this time.'

He walked across the silent room with great dignity, and I squelched along behind him.

The next day, while Flemynge was out riding on the estate, the vicar called. He was embarrassed, he said, although I could see no signs of it. The problem was – and he did hope I would understand – the Presscotts were well-loved in the neighbourhood. Would I mind, that is, he really must ask – Impatiently, I begged him to say exactly what he wanted of me.

I had invited him into the saloon where he was patently uncomfortable on one of the old settees, looking like a great black hippopotamus that has fallen into a pit. 'Miss Lucinda Presscott has asked that you and your husband not attend our parish church in future, Mrs Flemynge. Your recent ... ah ... residence in ... coupled with her bereavement, have made the poor young woman rather nervous.'

'Miss Presscott is seriously disturbed,' I said.

He agreed, choosing to give my words a different meaning. He was delighted that I understood, he said as he manouevred himself with difficulty to the edge of the settee. There were other churches in the vicinity, after all. He wagged a finger. Besides, my husband and I were not exactly diligent in our churchgoing, were we? Surely I appreciated that feelings were running rather high in the neighbourhood at the moment. My husband and I would be accepted in the community *eventually*, but just now –

I stood up and with the minimum of good manners assured the vicar I would not set foot in his church ever again. I escorted him to the door myself and closed it on him while he was still speaking. Several minutes later, I was still shaking with rage.

Later, when I told Flemynge about the request, he was as sensible of the insult as I, but seemed to have his emotions under better control. He had expected to be hated in these parts, he said, was accustomed to being despised by certain sorts of people. He felt that in many ways early rejection was a fine education for a young man. It stiffened the backbone.

I was not so strong, nor so self-reliant. 'Let us go away for a while,' I begged, suggesting London, thinking of its shops, theatres, crowded streets and the blessed anonymity that a great metropolis could bring. Flemynge would not hear of it.

'I will certainly take you away from Thorsby for a few days. It will not do for us to be here while everyone is mourning the death of old Presscott and attending his funeral. However, your nerves are not such that I would wish to tax you with a visit to London. I have been intending to visit Blakeney on the northern coast of Norfolk for some time. We will go there. Have you ever been to the seaside?'

'No, I haven't,' I said wearily. 'Is there anything to do in Blakeney? I have never heard of the place.'

'It has a most interesting salt marsh. Many unusual plants grow there.'

'Flemynge.' My voice shook. 'My nerves, about which you claim to be so concerned, will not support the tedium of looking at plants. I won't go!'

Despite my refusal and all my arguments, we were packed and on our way within two days. Flemynge had made a quite unnecessary to-do about my obtaining stout boots and sensible clothing. I would need nothing but the simplest of gowns to wear, he said, because we would be staying in a common inn, there being nothing grander in the area. I asked, sarcastically, if Millichip would accompany us. Flemynge, maddening in his good humour, said he thought I would be more comfortable if my maid were present to attend me.

Blakeney was about eighty miles from Thorsby, and since we were travelling in a chaise and four, we set off at a spanking pace. After ten miles, the splendid Thorsby horses were changed for two pairs of jobbers from a staging post, and from then on each stage saw us riding behind worse horses than the ones before.

The Crown and Anchor in Blakeney was indeed a rough inn, but the welcome we received at ten o'clock that night could not have been warmer. I was too tired to do more than follow the innkeeper's wife up the stairs to my chamber without so much as a 'good-night' for my husband. A strong smell of beer filled the inn; the voices of several fishermen drinking in the main parlour wafted up the staircase, and I smiled to think that I could scarcely understand a word they said.

The next morning, we met for breakfast in a small parlour and I had to admit that I had slept very soundly. I asked for and received approval of my strong boots and plain calico gown. Flemynge wore knee-breeches, a moleskin waistcoat, an open-necked shirt with a scarf knotted at the throat and labourer's high-low boots. He had a small metal box, about eighteen inches by eight, which he slung across his shoulders on a wide strap. It was for holding the plant specimens as we collected them, he told me. Tonight we would press those which were not too spongy to be satisfactorily pressed; the rest would need to be recorded with accurate drawings, carefully executed.

I said the prospect was thrilling.

Across the narrow road from the inn was what I presumed to be Blakeney Quay, but there was virtually no water. A stream meandered away into the distance to be lost among the low-growing plants, a haze of lavender dusting a beige prairie of weeds. Small ships lolled helplessly on the muddy banks, their masts pointing at odd angles. There were no sails; there was no sea.

'Where's the sea?'

'Almost a mile away, I suppose. The tide is out. Later these boats will be able to sail away. The landlord says the sea rises about thirteen feet between low tide and high tide.'

We crossed the road and, skirting the muddy banks, began walking through the shrubby undergrowth in the direction of the sea.

'Sea Lavender,' said Flemynge, pointing to the violet drift of flowers.

I stared out over the unpromising landscape, but soon had to lower my eyes as I followed Flemynge. The ground was wet, sinking slightly with each footstep. We had not gone a hundred yards before the hem of my gown was covered in mud, transferred from the undergrowth as I brushed past. Water had already entered my right boot.

'How far out do we have to walk to find some plants?' I asked.

'What do you think these are?'

'Weeds. Dirty, muddy, ugly weeds.'

Flemynge bent to snap off a stalk carrying small yellow flowers. 'This is not a weed. It is an important plant which grows only on marshland. It has a beauty of its own. Sea water covers these plants at high tide, yet they flourish here, whereas most plants would be killed if regularly covered by *clean* water, let alone *salt*-bearing sea water. That's what makes it interesting.'

I eyed it with distaste. 'What is it then?'

'Sea Purslane.'

'What? Doesn't it have a Latin name?'

'Yes, *Halimione portulacoides*. I want you to remember that.'

I laughed. 'I shall be doing well to recognize it as Sea Purslane. But tell me. When are we going to stop so that I can make some sketches? Does this muddy wilderness go on for ever?'

'At this very moment, we are doing what we came to do. I'll collect specimens as we walk along and you can draw them in comfort at the inn.'

'Hasn't your great artist friend been here before me?'

'Ferdinand Baur *is* a great artist. I became quite fond of him on our journey to the Antipodes, but so far as I know he has not recorded the plants of Blakeney marshes. I'm sorry you didn't benefit from studying his illustrations.'

'The man is a genius, to be sure, but I want to see the ocean. You promised me a visit to the seaside.'

'All right, we will visit the shore first. Then to work.' Flemynge consulted a roughly sketched map, checked the position of the sun, then indicated the direction we should walk.

I plodded on. My boots were covered in mud, my skirt was damp, and my legs and feet aching by the time we reached the top of a shingled ridge where I was able to catch my first sight of the sea. The day was clear, I could see for miles, nothing but water and the stately roll of the waves as they broke gently on the pebbled shore. Far, far out to sea a ship sailed past slowly. It was an impressive sight.

Despite the risk of acquiring more freckles, I removed my bonnet and immediately felt the sea breeze tear at my hair. The sun was hot on my face and a remarkable feeling of peace came over me. On that day, I fell in love with a view so majestic no work of art had ever done it justice.

Flemynge opened the parcel the landlord had given him. We made ourselves as comfortable as possible on the unwelcoming shingle and feasted in silence on bread, cheese and very warm claret.

'How excited you must have been to go to sea!' I said at last, licking my fingers.

'Yes, but I soon grew very tired of the sight of water. When you see nothing else for weeks on end, and the food is monotonous and the motion of the ship never ceases, the sea begins to lose its fascination. Are you rested? I would like to walk west on this ridge for a little way before we turn back to the inn. You would be wise to put on your bonnet. The sun will burn your skin.' He pulled me to my feet before gathering up the picnic remains.

I began trudging across the shifting stones, noticing how easily Flemynge walked on the difficult surface.

'Oh, look!' called Flemynge as he leapt halfway down from the shingle ridge on the landward side. 'This is Yellow Horned Poppy. Come, look at it. A most interesting plant.'

I followed him down gingerly, slipping and sliding

until I was standing beside him as he examined this single plant among the pebbles. The low clump was about a foot across, with fleshy bright green leaves, yellow flowers and pencil-thick protuberances tapering to a point.

'It's very attractive,' I said with surprise. 'I'd like to paint this one. This is the most interesting plant you've shown me. Can we take it back to the inn? I don't see why you must burden this dear flower with confusing Latin names when the English name describes it perfectly.'

'That's just the point. It's not a poppy, although the flowers bear a slight resemblance to poppies. It belongs to a different plant family. This is *Glaucium flavum*. Do you see the horn?' He snapped off a four-inch tapering section which came away cleanly. 'When the flowers fade, these seed cases form. Split it open lengthwise and you will see the seeds inside. When the cases are ripe, they burst naturally and the seeds are scattered. Even in this hostile environment, some will germinate.'

He picked a flower, a bud, a seed case and several leaves for his specimen box, but thoughtfully left the plant in place. I looked with fascination at the tiny glossy white seeds my fingernail had revealed. 'They're beautiful. I like to think of all these little seeds trying to grow here among the tumbling pebbles, with the sea pounding on the other side of the ridge. I think I can understand why you find plants so satisfying. I don't mean giving them difficult names or categorizing them. Plant families could never interest me. Just hunting for as many different plants as one could find and, well, *appreciating*.'

'If you hunt plants for any length of time, I predict you will wish to put them in some sort of order, will want to know which plant belongs where in the scheme of things. Come along. We'll look for something else. Sea Campion, I think. Keep your eyes open. It is low-growing and has small white flowers.'

Sea Campion was not difficult to find, nor were Sea Blite and Stonecrop, but Flemynge eventually noticed that my face was flushed and my breathing slightly laboured. Firmly, he turned me towards Blakeney and we began walking across the marshy ground that was considerably drier and, therefore, easier going than it had been earlier in the day.

'There's a church!' I said. 'Doesn't it look splendid with its tall square tower? And I can see some windmills.'

'That will be Blakeney church, I expect.'

'Oh, Flemynge, let us rest a while. I'll sit here. It doesn't matter about my gown. It's already filthy. I want to make some sketches. I want to draw the church from this angle and then see what I can achieve with a windmill. Do you mind? I'm so tired. I need to sit down for a while.'

He didn't mind at all. I settled down with a pad and pencils, and for several minutes he watched as I did half a dozen quick sketches of the church. Then the marsh called him, and he went away to see what he could find.

With his head down, walking at a snail's pace, he moved across the spongy ground. Twisting slightly, I drew Flemynge at work, just a few lines to indicate the curve of his spine, the sun beating down on his back from directly above, hardly any shadows at all.

He stopped suddenly, pulled at a plant, then turned to me excitedly. 'This isn't *Limonium vulgare*!'

'You amaze me!' I called back.

'You don't understand. This isn't the common Sea Lavender one would expect to find here. I suppose it could be *Limonium binervosum*. But that would be strange. Rock Sea Lavender is only common on the west coast of Britain. Perhaps it's a new discovery.' He shook his head, smiling a little, and put the sprig into his specimen box before carrying on his search. I turned my attention to the windmill.

At first, I could not think what was wrong, but I very soon realized I was sitting in a puddle. 'Water!' I shouted and scrambled to my feet. 'What's happening?'

Flemynge began running towards me. 'The tide's coming in! We must get out of the marsh. I'll come for you. Stay where you are.'

Cursing loudly, calling himself all kinds of fool, he crashed through the marsh, now and then stepping in fast-running sea water as it filled up each snaking channel and depression. I was marooned on a piece of ground which was already covered by an inch or two of water. A slurry of sea water and mud eddied past Flemynge's legs as he splashed towards me, his eyes searching the area, looking, I supposed, for safer ground.

I had never seen so much water in my life and knew nothing of the ways of the sea. In fright, I took several steps towards him. My foot sank in the ooze of a small channel, throwing me off balance. The current, amazingly strong, brought me down and I floundered. I could hear Flemynge shouting at me as my sketch pad floated away.

He reached me quickly, lifted me up, and with his arm around my waist, guided me back to my small island which was now almost a foot under water. I remembered that the tide rose thirteen feet. But how quickly? In the distance – a hundred yards or more – was the embankment which ran north from the town separating the marshland from the land which Flemynge had told me was now reclaimed meadow. The embankment must be safe, but how to get there?

'We must try for that patch of drier ground just over there,' said Flemynge. 'Ten yards away, no more. There is no way to reach it except by wading, but the current is treacherous, I warn you. We must not become separated. Put your arm around my waist and hold tight.'

I nodded as I slipped my arm around him to clutch a handful of shirt, then looked up, waiting for the signal to move. Our first few steps, taken in unison, went reasonably well, then I stepped into a hole. My feet made no contact with the bottom; I bobbed under the water like an apple in a barrel. Only Flemynge's strength and greater height kept me from floating away.

Occasionally, the water was too deep even for him. When necessary, he swam a few strokes, and inevitably we drifted downstream, away from our goal. We nearly missed the dry ground, but scrambled feverishly ashore, still clutching one another, too out of breath to say anything. And beneath our feet the dry ground began to soften with sickening speed.

He scanned the marsh and I watched his face, hoping for a clue to his feelings. Would we die? I had no way of knowing, except by his attitude, how desperate our situation was.

'Elinor, do you trust me? I shall be risking our lives on my knowledge of plant life, but I really think we have no choice.' He didn't wait for an answer. 'There! About twenty yards away. Do you see that patch of marsh grasses? That's *Puccinellia maritima* and *juncus maritimus*. Don't think me mad to be spouting Latin at such a time. The point is, those plants could not survive a twice daily wetting in salt water. Therefore, that piece of ground *must* be higher, must remain above the daily fluctuation of the tide. We should be safe there until the tide recedes. A long wait, I'm afraid.'

But a quick death, I thought, if he were wrong. I was surprised that any plants could survive being submerged twice a day, and so hadn't fully realized our danger. Nothing would have induced me to leave the quay if I had known.

'Hitch up your skirt to free your legs and take off your boots,' he said, already bending to untie his own.

I pulled up my skirt and finding no other means of securing it, tucked the hem into my bodice. My bonnet had slipped from my head and was now a dead weight, wet straw clamped to my back by ribbons that were throttling me. I tore at the ribbons in a frenzy and tossed the bonnet away, then bent to unbutton my boots, but the buttons and wet leather resisted my shaking fingers.

'Can't –' I managed to say.

Flemynge, whose own shoes were now dangling from his neck by their joined laces, stooped to help me. A minute of frantic activity saw us no closer to removing the boots.

'You'll have to wear them,' he said. 'I don't think they will hinder you too much. We can only make it to the raised ground over there by wading so we'll have to hope for the best. Can you swim?'

'I don't know,' I said foolishly, then: 'No, but I've read about it. I know the principle. You kick your feet and wave your arms, don't you?'

'More or less. We will hold hands and whatever happens you must not let go! And don't panic.' He gave a harsh laugh. 'Although why you shouldn't is beyond me. Now!'

We plunged in. Occasionally, he managed to get a foothold, treacherous, dissolving with the tide, but it helped. Sometimes we drifted helplessly in spite of our efforts at wading. We almost floated past the dry land, but Flemynge reached out and took hold of a clump of marsh grass and rushes. We floundered ashore, our wet clothing dragging against us. The embankment was now only sixty yards away, but there was no hope of reaching it until the water went down.

I began to laugh weakly. 'I'm so glad I married a botanist. Your knowledge has saved our lives.'

He was not to be comforted. 'We wouldn't have been out on the marsh if I weren't a botanist, and my foolishness nearly caused us to drown. Look at you.'

Tenderly, he pulled my skirt from the neck of my gown and wiped what he said was a most charming streak of mud from my face. 'My God, Elinor, I thought I was going to lose you today, before I had a chance to tell you I love you, and have done since I first saw you.'

'You can't have,' I said as he pulled me into his arms. 'I looked a fright that day.' He held me close as the muddy water swirled round us, clipping inches off our sanctuary with every passing second.

'*Halloo*!' came a voice from the distance. We looked in the direction of the embankment and broke apart in embarrassment.

A small crowd had gathered on the embankment, fishermen with wind-whipped cheeks, their aproned wives, and countless laughing children. One man, carrying a small boat on his back, was walking purposefully down the slope, further out towards the sea than where Flemynge and I were standing. When he judged himself to be at the right point, he launched the boat, took a pair of oars from his friend, and with great skill encouraged the little craft to drift to our island.

'Get yourselves in quickly,' he said, putting one foot on land. 'I can't hold it for long.'

Flemynge helped me into the boat without a word and climbed in after me. We sat on the narrow seat facing the oarsman as he pushed off and began to row us back to the quay.

'That was a fool thing to do,' said the man. He had a straggly brown beard and his clothes smelled vilely of fish. 'You would have drowned if I hadn't come for you. What were you doing out on the marsh, anyway?'

'Hunting for plants,' said Flemynge. 'It was very stupid of me to forget about the tide. We are most grateful. If you hadn't come for us, we would have had to stay there until the tide went out.'

'You wouldn't have lasted that long. You'd have drowned.'

'No,' I said with spirit. 'My husband knew that particular patch of ground would not be submerged because of the type of plants growing there.'

'Is that so?' said the man sceptically. 'If you think that, you should have been here at spring tide. That would have tested your idea. We thought you must be looking for gold when we saw you bent double staring at the ground like that. How come you didn't notice the water was coming in?'

'I was distracted,' said Flemynge. 'How did you know we were in trouble?'

The fisherman guffawed. 'Everybody what's got a telescope has been watching you this past fifteen minutes. A fine show.'

I covered my face with my hands and groaned, which spurred the oarsman to renewed laughter.

The quay was crowded. Several shallow-bottomed vessels were coming in on the tide, and men were waiting to unload larger ships, too. Women with pails of water stopped to gape, to tell each other what had happened and speculate about a disaster averted. There was almost a carnival atmosphere about the quay, a happy laughing mood engendered by the foolishness of foreigners. Mercifully, Millichip and Flemynge's valet were also there to meet us. Millichip held a cloak; Caxton had a blanket.

Flemynge helped me into the arms of the maid, before reaching into the pocket of his clinging breeches to fetch out a half crown for our grinning rescuer.

Ten minutes later, Flemynge knocked on my door, then entered before Millichip could remove even the first of my boots. She stood up, blushing, and with a laugh that strongly resembled a donkey braying, ran from the room. He smiled broadly at me as he turned the key in the lock.

# Chapter Eight

'Don't sit on the bed in those wet clothes, my love.' He pulled me to my feet.

'My shoes and stockings –'

'I'll take them off in a minute.'

I turned. 'Flemynge, the window –'

He laughed, but went to the window and twitched the skimpy red-checked curtains together, which scarcely reduced the light at all, yet bathed the small room in a rosy glow.

'What a fool I was not to have discovered the time of high tide. Can you ever forgive me? You may be sure that I will never be so careless of your life again.'

He had managed hooks, eyes and stubborn wet tapes with great skill, and now removed my gown, dropping it in a heap on the floor. Millichip had laid out a dry chemise for me; I snatched it up, indicating that he must turn round before I would take off the wet one.

'My shy wife! Very well. This time I will spare your modesty.' He kissed my forehead before taking a few steps away and turning his back to me.

For a moment, I stood dumbly, then looked away with something approaching panic when I saw that he was stripping off his shirt, the muscles of his back moving gracefully as he tugged it over his head.

'You had better be ready, because I'm turning round. It seems to me that I have some explaining to do.' He was wearing nothing but his breeches. 'I was angry and jealous of that man Dawnay. I said unforgivable things to you comparing you with my mother. I didn't believe it, not even when I was most angry and hurt. You are not at all like her, never have been. Can you forgive me?'

'Of course.'

'Kiss me and say the words. Show me what a fool I was to drive you from my bed that night.'

I raised my head; our lips met. The kissing was all his doing while I remained passive, remembering that I *had* climbed into his bed for the sake of my future, for money, for position.

Amazingly, he seemed not to notice that I was unable to give my heart or to speak of loving. I had never known him to be so happy as he called me 'beautiful', 'adorable', 'his own sweet love'. I submitted when he pulled me close, caressing.

'You thought I was insane. Admit it, Flemynge. You think I imagined Lucinda Presscott's visit –'

He stopped me with a kiss. 'I have never thought you were insane. I do believe you have been through a terrible ordeal which has strained your nerves. Unforgivably, I added another trauma today. As for the Presscott girl, we will see that the house is properly locked every night. Then she won't be able to get inside.'

'That's not the point, Flemynge. Listen to me. I want you to say –'

'Later, my darling, later.'

Gently, yet increasingly insistent, he bore me along on the tide of his desire as inexorably as the incoming sea had carried me away this morning. I felt my body respond, floating willingly towards new experiences.

But all the while, another Elinor – cold, unresponsive, incapable of loving – stood by, watching. I was two people: the one acting out her passion, the other observing the scene with sadness.

Later, lying in his arms, I fretted that he had no dry clothing in the room. What would he do? Put on his wet breeches, he said reasonably, and go next door to fetch dry clothes. But not yet. His tenderness unabated, he spoke of our future life, our happiness together, our oneness and the past spectre of his own loneliness.

I didn't speak at all, because I didn't know what to say, nor why I could not bring myself to reply with some conventional, if hypocritical endearment. He was so good to me, so kind and loving; he deserved some crumb of comfort, and yet, selfishly, I could not give it.

That night, I dreamed I was in the cellar of Chennings as the tide came in. This time, I knew there would be no rescue. I was going under, drowning. It was not to be, of course. Flemynge was there, his strong arms round me, protecting me from my night terrors, his soft voice bringing me fully awake with promises of his eternal nearness, promises that as our marriage progressed I would no longer have nightmares.

I ground my teeth, saying nothing even as I clung to him, avidly consuming all the comfort he had to offer. My nerves were *not* strained, I wanted to say. Nightmares were surely common to everyone. He slept again as soon as I was still and silent, but I lay locked in his arms for over an hour before I could drift into some more peaceful dream.

The week passed swiftly in idyllic weather: morning mists, burning mid-day sun, the still air of Blakeney contrasting with the tearing breezes of the shoreline, long light evenings spent walking or sketching followed by dark nights too short to refresh us after hours of lovemaking. It was a honeymoon most brides dream of, but have no hope of achieving.

What wife would not revel in a husband so patently in love that his eyes glowed with approval each time he looked at her? Flemynge spoke often of his love; he strove to amuse; he was disconcertingly alive to my every infinitesimal change of mood. Yet, for all his talk of our closeness, he continually failed to interpret the cause of my volatile disposition.

I almost hated him for persisting in regarding me as

some nervous invalid. His anger that night when I had come to his room had led to a quarrel between a man and a sane woman, and was easily forgiven. It was his constant concern, his watchful glances, his willingness to forgo his pleasure of the moment to protect me from tiredness or boredom or the least distress – these were the things I could not forgive, because of the attitude that lay behind them.

Feeling like a cold-hearted, ungrateful wretch, I tried especially hard to make amends by producing botanical drawings that would meet his exacting standards. But when some lifeless sketch mocked me from the paper, he always stopped me from throwing it away. Every line I drew was priceless, beyond criticism, according to my husband.

He rescued dozens of crumpled sheets, smoothing them out before slipping them into a folder along with the rest, be they good or bad. While, all the time, I saw swiftly concealed concern, a frowning moment before he would return to his role of ebullient lover, suggesting a walk or a game of cards or spillikens. But no, not spillikens since he had first noticed that my hands shook too much to make me a capable opponent.

Sometimes I felt I was in danger of being loved into my grave. So when the weather broke at last and the rains lashed the little inn and the wind raced chillingly across the flat marsh, I was very happy to let Millichip pack my bags so that we could return to the less intimate surroundings of Thorsby.

It was one of Millichip's duties to iron my finer gowns, rather than trusting them to the laundress. Two days after our return to Thorsby, she came to me as I sat reading in the saloon, with my favourite lavender gown clutched in her large red hands.

'Oh, ma'am, I ruined it! Whatever will you think of

me? I'm just no good at ironing these special things and that's a fact.'

I looked at the large burn on the front of the skirt. The iron had not just scorched its image on the fabric, but actually burnt a hole right through the gown. With a sigh, I considered what to do. It might be reclaimed by adding a false apron front, or the bodice might be removed from the rest and joined to a new skirt, but I had no heart to do either.

'Surely,' I said with some irritation, 'you were not so clumsy when working for your previous employer. Did you commit this sort of outrage often?'

'I never been a lady's maid before, Mrs Flemynge, nor never intended to be. Of course, I was happy to oblige Mr Flemynge when he came to our cottage to ask my father if he would let me work at the big house, but all the same –'

'Why did my husband choose you to be my maid?'

'Well, ma'am, he said there weren't much time to find a maid for you. Of course, there's Miss Somers what lives with her mother in the village. She was a lady's maid for years, but her last employer died and she's been home ever since. However, Mr Flemynge said he wanted a big strong young woman, and I must admit I'm all them things. Just the same, if you was to prefer Miss Somers, I wouldn't be at all offended. I know I'm useless. Mrs Hobson is always saying as much. Besides, my mam needs me at home to help with the cheesemaking and all. I love cheesemaking. And then there's the young ones. I have seven brothers and sisters much younger than me.'

'Millichip, you shall have your wish,' I said. 'Fetch Miss Somers to me, please, as soon as you can manage it. If I think she will suit me, you may leave immediately.'

Millichip did her best to look regretful about the gown and sorry to be losing her place, but succeeded only in looking overjoyed by her unexpected release from purgatory.

Somers was a delicate woman in her fifties, a good six inches shorter than I was, very neat, very cheerful and, I soon discovered, very knowledgeable about the management of clothing, the dressing of hair and the proper performance of the duties of a lady's maid. The tone of her mind was also far superior to Millichip's, and I thought she would offer me some much-needed companionship. I asked her to begin straight away and sent a note to Mr Stornaway, instructing him to give Millichip a quarter's wages and send her back to her family.

Flemynge received the news of Millichip's dismissal with polite interest. He really didn't seem to mind whom I employed as my personal servant. However, he took exception to my accusation that he had hired a *keeper* for me in the tall shape of the muscular Millichip.

'What would I know of lady's maids, Elinor? I chose someone whom I thought would serve you uncritically, no matter what state you were in when I fetched you from Chennings. I've heard that there is no snob to equal these grand personal servants, and that Somers' previous mistress was a marchioness. I hoped to spare you her condescension.'

I had chosen the worst possible time to confront him with my suspicions. We were in the bedchamber I now shared with Flemynge, in the very act of preparing to get into bed for the night. We slept beneath the ridiculous Polonaise canopy, and only a thick wall separated us from Somer's room. I had no idea how much she would be able to hear; I knew only that I could not hear *her* movements. Of all things, I didn't want her to know what we were saying, so I kept my voice low.

Flemynge, on the other hand, felt no such restraint. His deep voice filled the room as he told me that I was behaving like a fractious child looking for something to criticize, and wouldn't be satisfied if he could give me the moon on a string.

'Yes, I would,' I said instantly. 'I would be satisfied with a good deal less. I want to own the Old Manor House again. It's mine by rights. It was stolen from me and I want it back, so that I can visit it any time I wish. You could buy it for me if you really wanted to, but you won't put yourself to the trouble.'

There followed a terrible silence, long enough for me to feel satisfied in having aroused his genuine anger at last, and to wonder what Somers, no doubt pressing her ear to the door at this very minute, would make of our quarrel.

Flemynge ran his fingers through his hair with a weary sigh. 'If the Old Manor House will make you happy, I will move heaven and earth to buy it.'

'Oh, Flemynge!' I said, shaken with remorse. I had exhausted him with my moodiness, had certainly outworn his patience and might even have killed the very love that sustained me. I started towards him, arms outstretched. He turned his back and began putting on the dressing gown he had just removed, thrusting his feet into his slippers before looking at me with a sad smile.

'I will travel to Gloucestershire tomorrow and will probably be gone two nights. Since it will be necessary to leave the house very early in the morning, I'll sleep in my old room so that I won't disturb you.'

He went towards the door and I made no move to stop him, unable to offer a single reason why he should stay with me.

True to his word, he was gone before I woke the next morning. I breakfasted in my room, feeling no inclination to leave it. Somers had a pleasant voice and was full of plans for refurbishing a straw bonnet she had discovered in my cupboard. Her enthusiasm for her new post was limitless. For almost an hour, she held me a willing captive as she brushed my hair first one way and then another, suggesting ornaments I might purchase and hairstyles I might care to adopt on occasion. Since all her advice was interspersed with amusing stories about the women she had worked for in former times, the morning passed very agreeably. I told myself firmly that I didn't need Flemynge's company at all.

The trees were still dripping in a desultory way after heavy overnight rain. The sky was the colour of steel, making it the sort of day which is really best spent indoors with a lively companion discussing the latest fashions.

At twelve o'clock, Somers answered a knock on my chamber door, then stood aside to allow Mrs Hobson to enter. It was at once obvious that the two women disliked one another, which further endeared Somers to me.

'This message has been delivered from Essex Grange, ma'am. I am to wait for a reply,' said Mrs Hobson, handing me a single sheet of black-edged paper, weighed down with a large seal of black wax. Then she closed her lips firmly and folded her hands in front of her.

I read the note with considerable surprise.

> Dear Mrs Flemynge,
> I am empowered to make arrangements beneficial to yourself. If interested, please meet me at the dower house at one o'clock.
> 
> A.P.

'Who is A.P.?' I asked.

Somers gasped; Mrs Hobson smiled grimly. 'The note is from Mrs Presscott, ma'am. I am to wait for a reply. Are you willing to meet Mrs Presscott at the dower house?'

'So you have read the note?'

'Typical,' murmured Somers.

Mrs Hobson looked at the maid coldly. 'Barlow brought the note and told me what was in it. He has requested a word with you, Somers.'

'I will meet Mrs Presscott at the dower house at one

o'clock,' I said, and nodded my permission for Somers to go down to the servants' hall to see Barlow. The two women left together; I went directly to my wardrobe to choose something to wear for this strange meeting.

Somers returned a few minutes later. 'William Barlow is my cousin,' she explained. 'As you may know, he is the butler at the Grange now. I told him at the time he should not leave Thorsby, but after what happened, one of them had to go, I suppose.'

'Which? Who? What happened?'

'Why, my cousin asked Margaret Hobson to marry him, but she refused. The Presscotts are a strange family, to say the least, and William has been quite worn down by them. The old man was as cantankerous as they come towards the end. Half the time he couldn't recall William's name, although he'd been with the family for fifteen years. Then there's young master Aubrey. Very rackety and very expensive.' She lowered her voice. 'There's been talk for years about him and her.'

'*Him* and *her*?'

'Master Aubrey and Margaret Hobson. And her so much older. I told William he had a lucky escape there, but he doesn't see it that way, of course.'

'And the daughter?'

'Miss Lucinda? She's moody, strange. Keeps herself to herself, as they say. Her maid lives a terrible life, I hear. In fact, she is only twenty, but to my knowledge she has had three maids since she was fifteen.'

'Would you say she was deranged?'

Somers was scandalized. 'Oh, no! Nothing of that sort! Needs a good thrashing, if you ask me. That would soon stop her putting on airs.'

I studied Somers' cheerful face. 'I suppose you have known the Presscotts for many years. Now that my husband and I have come here as interlopers, you must find it strange working at Thorsby.'

'Not so odd, ma'am. The Presscotts are not well liked

in these parts. It's the general opinion that Mr Flemynge is the rightful owner of Thorsby.' She smiled brightly at me. 'And anyone can see you are getting better by the day. Now then. The weather is miserable. May I suggest you wear your plain linen and the green velvet spencer?'

I swallowed my anger and agreed. Why should I expect understanding from my maid?

The dower house had small pointed windows in the Gothic style, and since all of them were overshadowed by tall conifers, there must not have been a single room that ever received the sun. The house had a forlorn feel to it, and I could not imagine anyone living in it. In fact, I was fairly sure that no one *had* ever lived here.

Invisible from the main house, it had its own rutted drive leading from the public road. I had seen it before on one of my many lonely tours of the estate, had put my hands to the glass and peered through the dirty windows at the dusty rooms, finding it so uninteresting that I had never requested a key so that I might explore the inside.

On this day, I arrived early and toured the whole house. So it was that from an upstairs window I saw a plump lady, weighed down with black crepe and yards of veiling, picking her way with care along the puddled drive. I ran downstairs to greet her, relieved that my curiosity was finally to be satisfied. I could not imagine why she would want to speak to me.

She was wiping perspiration from her face with a black-bordered handkerchief as I opened the door. Her veil was thrown back, and she reacted as if I had caught her totally naked. The veil was quickly dropped; she greeted me coldly, and I invited her to step inside.

'I have arranged for two chairs to be brought here, and also some lemonade, so we may be comfortable while we talk.'

My hospitality seemed to displease her, but it was

hard to guess what thoughts were passing through her mind behind that thick veil.

In fact, Grimsby had not only seen to the arrangement of two chairs, but also a small table on which were placed a linen cloth, glasses, a large jug of lemonade and a plate of seed cake, thoughtfully covered by a napkin.

Mrs Presscott ignored it all and went directly to the french doors to stare out at the modest garden.

'Very clever of you,' she said bitterly.

'I beg your pardon?'

'Despite all these domestic touches, I want you to know I'm not here on a social visit. You cannot claim as much to your friends, if you have any. I would never call on you in a social way. Do you understand that?'

'And I would never invite you to my home, Mrs Presscott. Please remember, we are here at *your* request. I have not poisoned the lemonade, but just the same you are not obliged to drink any of it.'

To my surprise she sat down in one of the chairs without further fuss and indicated that she would like a glass of lemonade. I knew she regretted it instantly, however. She could hardly drink without raising her veil, and for some reason she didn't want me to read her expression. The filled glass remained on the table.

I was perfectly happy to play this game of wills, and removed the napkin from the cake which looked delicious. I was aware of Mrs Presscott's inner battle between greed and prudence as she stared at the cake. Greed won; she took a slice of cake, lifted her veil very slightly and slipped the cake up to her mouth. It was an absurd performance.

'I will return the furnishings of Thorsby.'

I started to ask why, but managed to say: 'When?' instead.

'Tomorrow.'

'All of them? Everything?'

'Everything but the furniture which is ours. I'm told

you have bought some tasteless pieces for the family quarters. You don't need our personal treasures.'

Now the battle was raging in my own breast. I wanted to ask her why she was taking this extraordinary action, yet I didn't want to give her the pleasure of hearing me beg for enlightenment. I tried, instead, to look unsurprised. Not an easy task.

'I am very pleased that you have taken this reasonable attitude, Mrs Presscott. The furniture, the paintings, the *objet d'arts* all belong to my husband. Everyone knows it.'

'Yes,' she said. The glass of lemonade disappeared behind the veil. 'But it would have been years before your husband could regain them if he went through the courts. Lawyers have cunning ways of delaying business.'

I drank my own lemonade slowly. Should I thank her? What attitude should I adopt? I was almost afraid to say anything for fear she would change her mind.

'But everything has its price,' she said, and I held my breath. 'Terrible things have happened to my family since your husband first set foot in the drawing-room of Thorsby. We have lost this estate which we regarded as our own, my husband has died, and soon the bank of Presscott and Stracey may be forced to close its doors. My son . . . Aubrey has his own plans. He owns Essex Grange, and I have no doubt that he will sell it very soon. He talks of moving to the Continent. Although it would be possible to live very cheaply there, I don't want to go. I had always thought that one day I would live in this house as a widow, when Aubrey brought a bride home to Thorsby. He will live abroad, but I see no reason why I should not come here just the same.'

'You want to live in the dower house?' I asked. 'Here, on the Thorsby estate? After all that has passed between your family and ours?'

'I don't see why not. This house was meant for me. I have a small pension, independent of Aubrey. I can be comfortable among the people I have always known. I was born just four miles from here. I am too old to learn to live among foreigners. I see no reason why you should object. Your husband will have his precious possessions about him. The dower house can't even be seen from Thorsby's windows. It has its own private drive. You will not know we are here.'

'*We*?' I asked blankly.

'Lucinda and I.'

There was no way that I could hide my shock. To have that girl actually on the estate would be terrible. I would never feel safe. And yet, how could I refuse to receive Thorsby's contents?

'My husband will be home again in a few days –'

'And my son will return home in a few days, also. Then it may be impossible to strike a deal. The decision must be yours, Mrs Flemynge, and you must make it now.'

'And, of course, you know that whatever bargain I make with you, Flemynge, as a man of honour, will keep.'

She sniffed disdainfully. 'He is too greedy to send the furniture back to us. Of that, I am certain. In any case, I have drawn up a document for you to sign.'

I took the single sheet of paper she handed to me and read it through carefully. It was brief.

> I, Elinor Flemynge, do hereby receive all of Thorsby's furnishings in return for allowing Mrs Amanda Presscott and her daughter, Miss Lucinda Presscott, to live at the dower house during the course of their lifetimes.

The document was totally lacking in those confusing legal terms that littered the pages of more formal agreements. But why not? It said all that was necessary. I quickly scribbled my name, afraid that if I hesitated, I might change my mind.

'I must hurry,' said Mrs Presscott as she folded the paper and stuffed it carelessly into her reticule. 'The carters have been engaged. The furniture will come to you tomorrow.'

'May I send you home in one of Thorsby's carriages?'

'Certainly not. My coachman is waiting for me at the bottom of the lane. I am a woman of my word, Mrs Flemynge. A woman of honour. I depend upon you to show your husband where his best interests lie. He will be shunned by everyone if he fails to honour this agreement.'

'And you must tell your son that you have done a sensible thing today. Too much of his energies was being wasted in futile longing for Thorsby. I'm sure he will be happier now that the business is finally settled.'

Mrs Presscott laughed bitterly, and without another word left the dower house.

The next day, all the servants, and some of the cottagers, helped to get the furniture into place. The return of Thorsby's rightful furnishings seemed to be reason enough for general rejoicing, and by nightfall, most of the cottagers and several members of the indoor staff were merry on Thorsby's home brew.

I had been elated at first, but began to feel isolated from the celebrations. Thorsby, empty, had been a strange house, well suited to an unconventional husband and wife. Thorsby, furnished, was a very grand establishment indeed, almost a palace with its formally arranged furniture, priceless paintings and Chinese vases. The saloon, in particular, was dazzling. I avoided it.

The last ornament was in place by half past ten that night. Margaret Hobson, very much in charge with her household keys rattling at her side, seemed to be in the throws of some quasi-religious experience. Her face glowed with inner happiness as she made obeisance to Hepplewhite and Sheraton, Claude, Lely and the lesser portrait painters. She was tireless in directing the army of helpers to put each chair, cabinet and table in its allotted place, but as the day wore on and Thorsby took on its old appearance, she became increasingly cool to me. There was a hint of insolence, as if she thought the Flemynges were not good enough to possess such treasures. By the time the house was ready to be shut up for the night, we were being excessively polite to one another, and I thought I had lost a battle I hadn't known how to fight.

The sparsely furnished bedroom I now shared with Flemynge had not escaped the general aggrandisement. Before I knew what they were about, several men had dismantled the Polonaise bed and taken it away to another room. A rich Chinese carpet of blue with a border of flowers had been spread across the floor, and on it the men had placed a spectacular bed. I had never seen one like it. In the style of Thomas Chippendale, they told me, with gold damask and Chinese silk hangings and crowned by a carved gilded cornice on nine-foot bedposts. The bed was fully six feet wide and had its own special bed linen. I thought I would get lost among all those plump pillows, especially tonight when Flemynge was away.

The carpet in the dining-room was Turkish or perhaps Persian. I wasn't sure. The mahogany dining table stood on four pedestals and without its leaves was (the servants said with almost personal pride) sixteen feet long if it was an inch. The thought of presiding over a gathering of such size and magnificence as would be needed to honour this table made me feel queasy.

In the library I felt a little more at ease, because the books had been there from the first. The addition of library tables and well-upholstered leather chairs added to the comfort of the room without changing its character. It was very late; I had brought a lamp with me and left instructions that the door to the main house be left unlocked so that I could let myself in after the staff had gone to bed. I wanted to find something to read and perhaps grow accustomed to this one room before facing the mighty bed.

The old library table had been banished. Someone had taken the contents of its large drawer and dropped them, higgledy-piggledy, on the leather surface of the original desk. I decided to sort the papers neatly into piles by subject, assuming all the papers and pamphlets to be connected with botany in some way, and in fact many of the papers were about plants. I put these first twenty or thirty sheets to one side and turned my attention to the remainder.

On the top of the pile was a handsomely produced treatise, *Description of the Retreat* by a man named Samuel Tuke, which outlined the moral methods of treating the insane in his grandfather's Yorkshire madhouse for insane Quakers. I read the entire work at a gallop before setting it aside. It seemed to be a humane establishment – no whipping, chaining or dosing – but just reading about a madhouse shortened my breath and gave me a pain in my chest.

It was stupid of me to pick up the next treatise, *Observations on the present state of the York Asylum*. York Asylum, I quickly discovered, was very different from The Retreat: badly run, the physician in charge given to lining his pockets and treating his patients by means of bleeding and the evacuants. One patient, I read, had the itch very badly, was extremely filthy, his health so much impaired he was not able to stand by himself, his legs very much swelled, one of them in a state of mortification.

I sat back in the library chair and closed my eyes, waiting for the nausea to wear off. Why did Flemynge want to have such grim reading material in the house? I wanted to forget about madhouses. Didn't he know that? And here I was, faced with the gruesome stories of unfortunate people I had never met, whom I could not help, but about whom I felt morbidly compelled to inform myself.

Like a Lascar taking up his opium pipe, I reached out with a shaking hand and turned the page.

'. . . one patient without any clothes whatsoever, standing in a washhouse on a wet stone floor apparently in the last state of decay'. This description was by the same Samuel Tuke who had described his family's Quaker Retreat. Cleverly, he had managed to become a governor of York Asylum (thereby becoming one of the few sane people allowed to enter it) by paying a donation of twenty pounds. 'The patient was removed to a suitable part of the asylum, where he was better attended, and in a few months was so much recovered as to be removed to his parish in an inoffensive though imbecile state.'

My imagination provided me with a vivid picture of the imbecile. I could smell him and hear him muttering, the way old Barty at Chennings used to do before he died. I, too, had experienced this imbecile's sense of helplessness in the face of brutal imprisonment. Or was he too mentally impaired to suffer as I had done?

'I will not read any more,' I said aloud, aware that the house was silent, and the servants very likely in bed. But there was very little more to read, and since my willpower had deserted me, I knew that whatever the cost to my nerves, I would read on. The last piece of paper in the stack was a handwritten letter.

Making a great effort to control my turbulent emotions, I dried my eyes and studied the neat writing. The letter was from The Retreat in Yorkshire, addressed to Flemynge and dated just a few days previously. I read the signature first and saw that it was from the very active Samuel Tuke.

My dear Fitzroy Flemynge,

My most humble apologies for any distress I may

have caused thee. But please remember that I never said thy wife was insane, merely that it was highly likely. How could I make a positive diagnosis when I have never met her? I am not qualified to pass judgement on the mental health of anyone. I did suggest that Mrs Flemynge should be seen by a physician. Yet I do understand thy reluctance to do such a thing, especially in the light of recent revelations about the physicians attached to some of our larger public asylums. Believe me, I am delighted to learn of thy wife's mental state and wish thee both a long and fruitful life.

> Thy affectionate friend
> Samuel Tuke

I dropped the letter on the desk, put my head in my hands and cried, not knowing why I cried. After all, this letter proved Flemynge believed I was sane. In the teeth of authoritative advice, he had refused to have me examined by a physician who might well have quacked me to death with green and grey pills. Still I cried, haunted by memories of Chennings.

I wanted with all my heart to leave the library with its tales of horror, but was afraid to walk alone all the way back to the bedroom. I thought about ringing for a servant. Just a few steps would bring me to the bell-pull, but pride prevented me from taking those steps. I would not admit to anyone that I was so foolishly afraid.

I stood and picked up the lamp. Don't think, move quickly and don't stop for anything, that was the way. I almost ran along the colonnade, entering the main house by a side door which I locked behind me with feverish haste. Up the stairs I flew, the lamplight flickering madly, and into our room.

Somers had laid out a gown on the new bed, the windows were shuttered against the night; the thick carpet smothered my footsteps. This room, at least, had been made more beautiful. I would grow used to its splendour, and pictured Flemynge here, preparing for bed, our private world now enriched by these beautiful possessions.

Undressing quickly, I slid into the large bed, curling up like a kitten on my side, then stretching out on my back and wiggling my toes. The bed was unbelievably comfortable. I thought I would be able to sleep tonight after all.

But first I must reach out to the lamp and turn down the wick, extinguishing that comforting glow. Gritting my teeth, I plunged the room into darkness, and the bitter smell of lamp-oil mocked my fears. Every sort of menacing sound reached me from beyond the shuttered windows, banging and knocking and rasping, but I fought my imagination until physical tiredness overcame mental turmoil and I slept.

# Chapter Nine

All morning I kept my ears pricked for the sound of Flemynge's carriage. In the event, he drove straight to the stables and entered our private quarters through the servants' door. He caught me by surprise as I was sketching an arrangement of fruit, and welcomed me into his arms when I threw down paper and pencil and so far forgot the angry words that had passed between us as to leap at him with a cry of delight.

'What's going on here?'

'All the furniture has been returned to Thorsby.'

He was as surprised as I had hoped he would be, but not quite as overjoyed as I had expected. He wanted to know exactly how all this had come about. Bravely, I told him about Mrs Presscott and the document I had signed, admitting that I hadn't been given a copy.

As I had feared, he objected strongly to having Mrs Presscott and Lucinda anywhere at all on Thorsby's grounds. He admitted that he would have to honour the agreement, and reminded me that I would not enjoy having that strange girl living so near to us. He was quite certain that Mrs Presscott had arranged it all without her son's knowledge, although, for the life of him, he couldn't think why. He said there must be many houses she could move into which would not have such painful associations for her.

Before I could reply, Grimsby entered with a decanter of madeira and two glasses on a silver tray.

'I thought you might like to refresh yourself, Mr Flemynge,' said the young butler, beaming. 'And perhaps celebrate the return of Thorsby to its proper glory.'

'Very thoughtful of you,' said Flemynge. 'I have not yet recovered from my surprise.'

Emboldened, Grimsby tucked the tray under one arm and stood at ease. 'I've had a long discussion with Mrs Hobson, sir, and we feel the staff is just too small to manage the furnished house properly. More chambermaids are what's needed. Four or five of them. Must keep everything in perfect condition. This is the finest house for miles around. And, of course, you will be wanting to entertain now the house looks as it should, and nobody can doubt you're the proper owner.'

Flemynge toasted me silently with his glass before answering Grimsby. 'Give me time to catch my breath and look about the house. I'll give you my answer tomorrow.'

'Thank you, sir. It's a pleasure – if I may say so – to hold a position in such an establishment, not that I ever listened to what people said about . . .' He stopped, blushed, then bowed himself out of the door.

Flemynge was amused. 'Grimsby has not spoken so much to me since Stornaway engaged him. I think I have passed the test of ownership.'

I swallowed my disappointment when he told me that the Baker family, who had bought my estate, were still determined to hold on to the Old Manor House. My dream seemed to be as far off as ever, despite Flemynge's reassurances. 'Every man has his price, but that price cannot always be counted in pounds, shillings and pence. We shall see. In the meantime, I would like to become acquainted with the home we do possess.'

Together we went on a tour of the house, and as each room was inspected in turn, Flemynge's spirits seemed to sag just as mine had done. When we reached the library, he put his arm around my waist. 'I can't help feeling it is a change for the worse. What have we done?'

'Made the servants very happy.'

'The saloon is no longer habitable. I preferred it the way it was.'

'I know. And oh, Flemynge, the paintings! I feel so intimidated by all the masterpieces on the walls that I haven't the audacity to take my sketch pad into the room. All those gilded chairs! Did you know? Each one has its accustomed place. But it will be too cold to sit in there during the winter whatever the furnishings.'

Flemynge was happier about our bedroom. I ordered supper to be served there and had two dozen candles lit. Wall sconces and candelabra cast a romantic glow. We ate very little and went to bed early.

Some hours later, I was disturbed by the sound of shutters being opened. Fully awake in an instant, I threw back the covers, determined to go downstairs and prevent Lucinda Presscott from leaving the house until I could prove to everyone that she really did visit Thorsby regularly.

But I didn't manage to leave the bed. Flemynge's arm snaked out to catch me about the waist. He pulled me back against him and refused to loosen his grip.

'You are not going downstairs, Elinor. There is no one there. Go back to sleep. Try to put all ugly thoughts out of your mind.'

'Let me go!' I tugged at his arm, and tried to reach his fingers to pull them backwards so that he would be forced to release me. 'You won't stop me from having ugly thoughts this way. I'll prove to you that I'm not insane.'

'How many times do I have to tell you? I never believed you were insane!'

'Oh, no,' I said. 'But you consulted Samuel Tuke about me, and he thought I was mad, didn't he?'

'How do you know about my visit to Samuel Tuke?'

I kicked backwards several times, hoping to catch him on the shins, but he was adroit at moving beyond my reach, and very soon the bedclothes were in a tangle. He allowed me to struggle until I was out of breath.

'Now then, Elinor. I want an explanation. How do you know about Samuel Tuke?'

'The old desk in the library. I sorted the papers from it and put them away in the proper Thorsby desk last night. Who is he? That is, I know about The Retreat. I read Tuke's essay on the moral methods of treating the mad and on the work of his grandfather's establishment. But why did you discuss me with him?'

'That is a long story and to make you understand, I must start at the very beginning. If you promise not to try to get out of bed, I will let you go.'

I promised; he released me, and together we plumped up the pillows to sit side by side. It was totally dark in the bedroom. I could not see my husband at all, but I felt his sinewy thigh next to mine and was aware of the calm steadiness his presence usually gave me. The thick Chinese carpet swallowed up the hollow sound that had once been a feature of this room. Flemynge's deep voice carried no further than my ears as he recounted his emotions on first visiting Chennings.

'I had cynically agreed to be a magistrate, aware that my position as owner of Thorsby was entirely responsible for the invitation. I remember very well that I had no enthusiam for inspecting Chennings, but did so because Colonel Sotherby asked me to do it.

'It was a sobering experience. I witnessed the depths of human misery, saw the suffering caused by supposedly humane people in the name of caring. I also saw a young girl with bright blue, brave eyes who begged me to free her.

'My life at that time was in something of a turmoil. For several years, I had been saving every penny I could earn so that one day I might open a nursery and sell plants. I needed five hundred pounds, and the prospect of collecting such a sum was remote. Then, almost overnight I acquired Thorsby and an income of five thousand. As owner of this house it was no longer suitable that I should open a nursery, much less work alongside my employees. Miss Makin had some weeks earlier refused my offer of marriage and married a baronet soon after. I was alone in the world, without a purpose, without direction. By the greatest good fortune, I left Chennings that day knowing two things: I intended to marry you, and I was determined to devote my life to making you happy.

'I left you here, you will remember, and travelled to York to sell some property. While I was in the vicinity, I visited The Retreat and saw for myself how humanely and, incidentally, how successfully the Quakers treat their insane.

'After he had shown me all round The Retreat, Samuel Tuke asked me why I had come to him. What, if anything, had prompted my interest in the insane? Naturally, I told him about you.

'He was at once sceptical. It was a common delusion among the insane, he said, that they have been improperly imprisoned by relatives who covet their fortunes. I told him I did not doubt your story for one moment. Later, after I had spoken to your aunt, I wrote to tell him that my faith in you had been vindicated. You have read his reply.'

'But you never told me any of this! If you believed I was sane, why didn't you tell me about your visit to The Retreat when you came home?'

'Because I –'

'Because you weren't quite sure.' I said. 'Well, you can forget all this nonsense about the insane. I don't want you even to think about insanity. It is always on your mind, distorting your view of everything. You are obsessed by it and it must stop.'

'Elinor!' He put his arm round my shoulders and held me close until my sobs ceased and I could be reasonably calm again. I had cried to the point of exhaustion and now weakly agreed to slip down in the bed and go to sleep if possible.

I turned on my side, away from him, and almost

immediately his arm encircled my waist once again. I strained every nerve to lie still within his imprisoning embrace until the even sound of his breathing told me he was asleep.

Only then did I venture to move very carefully from his grasp, out of the bed, into the hall, and, finally, with great stealth into the saloon. By leaving the door to the hall fully open, I had just enough light to see that the terrace doors and shutters were closed as they should be.

With a thudding heart, I stumbled over to the hidden door and pulled it open, to feel about in the inky darkness with a trembling hand, before closing the door again.

No one had come stealthily into this room except myself. I had to admit I had been mistaken; Lucinda Presscott had not entered Thorsby tonight after all. For the first time, I experienced genuine doubts about the other occasion.

Running up the stairs in my bare feet, I opened the bedroom door and hurried into bed, to be met with open arms by my wakeful husband who comforted me without words, more importantly without words of reproach. I could not get close enough to him, clutching him fiercely as I tried to shut out the dreadful thoughts that had followed me up the stairs. And all the while, I wondered why it was that I found his nearness so reassuring, when it was surely his obsession with madness that caused me so much distress.

Several days later, Grimsby brought two letters into the breakfast room just as we were finishing a substantial meal of ham and scrambled eggs. Flemynge read the first letter and then told me that his Uncle Alfred and Cousin Caius had invited themselves for a visit, and would be arriving on the following Monday.

I was far from pleased, anxious about how to entertain two men for several weeks when we were scarcely on friendly terms with our neighbours. Flemynge could hardly have heard a word I said, because he was carefully reading the second letter.

I watched him fold it along its original creases and slip it into his coat pocket without referring to it.

'Is the letter about my estate?' I asked.

'No, dear.'

'From Samuel Tuke, then. Have you had another letter from him?'

'It is from Mr Brown. I travelled to the Antipodes as his assistant, you may remember. He often writes to me.'

'I didn't know,' I said. 'Why does he write? Has he asked you to go on another expedition? Will you go away?'

'Don't be absurd. Of course I won't go away.' With a sigh of resignation, Flemynge removed the letter from his pocket and read it aloud to me.

> 'My dear Fitz,
> Thank you for your letter of the tenth inst. You will be disappointed to learn that the specimen you sent me is *Limonium bellidifolium*. Rare on the north coast of Norfolk, as you mentioned, but not unknown.

'That is all he has to say. Not very interesting.'

'Why will you be disappointed to learn the name of a plant?'

'Well, because if it had been unknown and unnamed –'

'You could have named it!' I cried. He shrugged. 'Could you have called it after yourself? *Limonium flemyngium?*'

'*Flemyngei*. Yes, but I doubt if I would have done so. Rather arrogant, don't you think?'

'You were very excited when you discovered that rare plant. Yet we talked for hours about all sorts of things after that day when the tide came in. Why didn't you tell me of your hopes concerning the plant? You don't want to share your interests with me, do you?'

'Why should I share such a faint hope? It was all vanity anyway. If the plant had been a new one, if I had been given the privilege of naming it, I promise you, I would have said so immediately. Surely, one's wilder daydreams need not be shared. I'll be in the library if you need me.'

He left the room, and I slumped in my chair, wondering why I persisted in being such a shrew. When I heard Flemynge call Grimsby's name, I jumped to my feet and reached the door in time to hear Flemynge instruct that letters should be delivered to him only when he was alone in future, so as not to agitate Mrs Flemynge.

We chose to greet Uncle Alfred and Caius in the saloon. We had grown accustomed to the room fully furnished, and besides, we thought this was the perfect place to meet our first house guests formally.

Uncle Alfred, a tall slim man with a thick head of dark hair just beginning to turn grey at the temples, seemed considerably surprised to be shown directly into this room, and said so. He had a kindly face which broke into a smile easily. Laughter lines enhanced his fine eyes. I liked him before he had even crossed the room to take Flemynge's hand in both of his.

'Well, Fitz, dear boy. It is splendid to see you here at Thorsby where you belong. Just as it should be, old chap. So this is my new niece, Elinor.' Uncle Alfred not only took both my hands in his, but gave me a warm kiss on the cheek. 'The whole county speaks of your beauty, my dear.'

'The whole county hasn't seen me,' I said, but Uncle Alfred was still talking.

'Allow me to introduce Caius, my good-for-nothing son. Come, lad and meet your cousins.' Uncle Alfred spoke with so much warmth that it was no wonder Caius allowed himself to be described in such terms without a flicker of annoyance.

I could trace a certain resemblance between the cousins, something about the deep-set eyes and strong chins. Caius looked ten or fifteen years younger than Flemynge, although I knew there was no more than five years between them. Flemynge's face hinted at earlier suffering, and perhaps showed signs of the years he had spent travelling to and from the Antipodes. Caius's face was unlined; nothing had as yet been written on his features. He seemed to be a gentle young man with something of his father's warmth, though nothing at all of his parent's confidence and vivacity.

'By Jove!' exclaimed Caius, looking round him. 'What a superb painting!' He walked over to a lacquered commode and bent forward the better to see a gold-framed painting showing an extremely plain, sparsely furnished interior. 'It's a Pieter de Hooch, surely,' he said. 'A Dutch interior. Late seventeenth century. My father has two paintings by the same artist.' He turned to face me. 'I believe you are an accomplished water-colourist.'

It didn't surprise me that he knew about my hobby. Father and son obviously had devoted spies. 'No, no. I dabble only, I assure you. When I was younger I was too lazy to apply myself, and now regret it.'

Caius's attention had fallen on a blue and gilt vase. 'Ah, my father told me about the Coalport vase. May I?'

I nodded and Caius picked it up with great care, turning it round to study each of the four scenes painted on the sides. 'Magnificent. My father says my great-grandfather disposed of his entire collection of Coalport shortly before he died. All except this piece. Such a pity.'

'If you are not too tired after your journey, would you care to take a tour of the house?' I said, and thought I read pleasure in Flemynge's eyes when Caius and Uncle Alfred agreed with enthusiasm.

The tour progressed at a snail's pace. Uncle Alfred had some extended reminiscence concerning each room we entered, while Caius carefully studied and commented upon every item, no matter how small. He identified the paintings, speaking of the artists as if they were old and much admired friends.

The moment we entered the yellow drawing-room, Uncle Alfred said 'Good God!' and strode directly up to a small, indifferently executed painting of a young woman posed traditionally in a white muslin gown, wide blue sash and chip-straw bonnet. 'I expected Hildebrand to have destroyed this one,' said Flemynge's uncle. 'Don't tell me it has been hanging just there all these years.'

'I brought this one down from the attic just the other day,' said Flemynge. 'I don't suppose the Presscotts even remembered having put it there. It seemed to be the proper thing to do, although the painting is a poor representation, I believe.'

'There, Caius,' said Uncle Alfred solemnly, 'is the only likeness of your Aunt Joanna in existence. My father, I am ashamed to say, destroyed every last drawing of her, even one I sketched as a lad.'

I drew in my breath and glared at Flemynge. How dare he hang a painting of his mother without even telling me! I moved a little closer and studied the face of the hateful Joanna, happy to find no resemblance between mother and son.

When we went upstairs, I led them first to the bedroom I shared with Flemynge. 'And this is our room.'

'What, the state bedroom?' exclaimed Uncle Alfred, laughing. 'And why not? You won't be entertaining the King, after all. Especially since he is mad as . . . No, no, I believe a home should be lived in. Beautiful possessions are meant to be enjoyed, not shut away.'

'Isn't that a Rembrandt cartoon?' asked Caius, peeping over my shoulder.

'I believe so,' I said and shut the door. Flemynge was beginning to look very grim, and I felt like the perfect fool. Mrs Hobson, or *someone*, should have told us this was the state bedroom.

We dined that evening in the small dining-room, seated at a modest table which was dominated by a two-foot-high silver épergne. I had thought the piece would be very attractive filled with fruit and flowers, but it merely made the table appear to be top-heavy – just as Mrs Hobson had said it would.

The food tasted of nothing in particular to me; my nerves had destroyed my appetite. I knew, nevertheless, that Chef had prepared a brilliant dinner for the guests. Uncle Alfred and Caius did not pass up a single dish. When the third course was set upon the table and Caius chose roast grouse, with bread sauce as well as vol-au-vent of greengages, which he followed with fig pudding, I began to feel a little queasy. I had been eating sparingly, but stopped altogether when Flemyge's uncle began to talk about Joanna.

'You have had years in which to feel hard done by, Fitz, and I can't say I blame you. Your life has been harder than it should have been, and I am pleased and proud that you have shown such strong character in overcoming your misfortune.

'But I ask you to spend a moment looking at past events from your mother's point of view. For some reason, my parents never liked Joanna. Extraordinary way for a mother and father to behave, but that is how it was. Everything she did was wrong. I never heard them say one affectionate word to her. Then the marriage to Presscott was arranged and she kicked up a fearful dust. Well, she was very young, but I was even younger. I must admit I thought she was overdoing the complaints, and we fell out. The wedding was a miserable affair. For one thing, Presscott never had his fair share of relatives. Almost all the guests were on our side.'

Uncle Alfred helped himself to some more fig pudding from the dish offered to him. 'By the time Hildebrand and Joanna returned from their honeymoon, they could hardly hide their hatred of one another. She had a quiet word with me. I won't say much in present company, but he was a damned queer fish. Damned queer.'

'My mother spoke of it often,' said Flemynge.

'Did she, by George! Shouldn't have. I used to call her Moaning Minnie. Anyway, when she ran off with that ... with your father, we were all furious. Terrible scandal. Very embarrassing. She never knew it, but I was responsible for getting my father to make her a small allowance. He didn't want to do it, but I told him she might otherwise get into further scrapes to support herself after Buckland died. My father promised to disinherit me if I ever wrote or spoke to her. We had lost Thorsby; I meant to hang on to Higgleton Great Hall. I behaved shabbily towards you and I regret it now. But by the time Parliament had passed an act enabling Hildebrand to divorce her, I was sick of the sound of my sister's name. That sort of business provides hours of amusement for every yokel in the country.'

'I know she suffered,' said Flemynge. 'I have heard all of this before, I assure you.'

Uncle Alfred nodded sadly. 'The woman was *born* bitter. She really ought not to have burdened her child with all that business, but never mind. Justice has been done at last. Thorsby is in your hands. And if you are wondering why my father would refuse to claim an estate like this just to punish his daughter, all I can tell you is, that's the sort of man he was. Now then,' he smiled at Elinor. 'Not another word will I speak about the whole sorry affair.'

Caius, who had kept his eyes on his plate throughout his father's speech, now looked up, apparently anxious to change the subject.

'I understand you went to the Antipodes with Robert Brown. Where exactly did you visit?'

'Apart from New Holland itself,' said Flemynge, 'the southern portion of Van Diemen's Land. We were gone four years and returned to Liverpool in October of 1805. My part in the expedition was a humble one. I helped to press some of the four thousand specimens we collected under Mr Brown's direction.'

'It must have been a great adventure,' said Caius. 'I'm no botanist, I'm afraid, but some of my friends dabble a bit. They took me to meet Sir Joseph Banks, and that's where I met Mr Brown who is now his librarian, as you know. Brown didn't speak of his travels. I was amazed when Father told me a few weeks ago that my own cousin had been a member of the famous expedition.'

'I may have just missed you,' laughed Flemynge. 'After we returned from the Antipodes, I worked on Mr Brown's *Prodromus Florae Novae Hollandiae*. The plants were drawn by the great Ferdinand Baur, you know. It was very important work. It's not surprising that Mr Brown was extremely disappointed by the poor sales. Then in 1810, Sir Joseph appointed Mr Brown as his librarian, and we parted company, although he made it possible for me to join several much shorter expeditions. It has been a privilege to know him.'

'How did you happen to join the expedition to New Holland, my boy?' asked Uncle Alfred.

'As you may know, Captain Flinder's ship, the *Investigator*, sailed from Portsmouth. Sir Joseph Banks had recommended that Mr Brown be taken along as naturalist. Brown put up at the Golden Lion in Portsmouth several days before the ship was due to sail. I had arrived at the inn three days earlier – as boot boy.'

'Good Lord, Fitz, I never realized things were so desperate for you,' said Uncle Alfred.

'I . . . living with my mother had become intolerable. I

left home and travelled round the south of England doing whatever I could. After about three weeks, I reached Portsmouth with five shillings in my pocket. Not all my jobs were so humble as the one at the Golden Lion.'

'Portsmouth must have been a rather dangerous place for a young man,' said Caius. 'Weren't you afraid of being pressed into the Navy?'

'It hadn't occurred to me when I arrived, but I soon learned to fear the press gangs. However, when I realized which Mr Brown was sleeping upstairs and what he was about to do, I approached him and begged a place on board. Botany was my passion even in those days, and I managed to impress him with my knowledge and willingness to work hard. I just had time to write a brief letter to my mother before we sailed.'

'And so you had a glorious adventure and some training in an exacting discipline. All good preparation for your present position,' said Uncle Alfred.

'Do you think so? I rather feel my studies are wasted.'

'Not at all, Fitz. You are in a position now to fund your own expeditions. You could send men to the other side of the world.'

'Yes,' said Flemynge. 'In a position to patronize men with ten times my knowledge and intelligence, act as paymaster for others to have grand adventures while I sit at home.'

And so it was that in five minutes, Uncle Alfred had discovered more about Flemynge's past than I had. But then, Uncle Alfred was not so self-absorbed as I was. Shame kept me silent throughout the remainder of the meal.

I had been worried about how to entertain our guests, but over the next few weeks, they seemed to make their own amusements during the days, preferring to be alone with us in the evenings. Uncle Alfred's first interest was the stables. He gave quantities of unwanted advice about the animals Flemynge should have in his possession and tried to persuade his nephew to travel with him immediately to Tattersall's in London to purchase a few horses.

When this proposal failed, he turned his attention to me, telling me I must learn to ride. To my surprise, Flemynge agreed. A suitable horse was purchased locally and Uncle Alfred began to instruct me. He was a talented and patient teacher, tempering his criticisms with humour and anecdotes about his late wife's considerable riding skills that made me laugh just when I ought to be concentrating. I enjoyed the lessons very much as summer slipped into autumn and the countryside exchanged shades of green for warmer colours.

Although Flemynge and I asked ourselves each night how much longer our guests would remain, we found the company invigorating. Uncle Alfred's affection for us both could not fail to please. Caius and Flemynge discovered many similar interests. I had never seen my husband so relaxed.

Then one morning I rose feeling very sick, and managed to reach the commode just in time. When I returned to the bedroom, Flemynge was waiting for me with a quizzical look.

'What do you suppose is the matter?' he asked.

'We both know,' I said, smiling at him. 'Do say you're pleased.'

'Of course I'm pleased, but now I wish my uncle and Caius would go home. You will not want to continue with a houseful of guests.'

I lay down on the bed and put an arm across my eyes. 'I don't suppose it matters if they stay a week or two longer, but I'm a poor hostess. I can't eat breakfast this morning. I wonder how long I will continue to feel this way. The Maltbys are coming to dine tomorrow night, but presiding over a dinner of several courses is too terrible to think about just now.'

Mrs Hobson's eyebrows had risen so far they were almost lost in her hairline, but I stuck to my original plan. We would dine with the Maltbys in the large dining-room. I asked if something could be done to shorten the length of the table which would be rather long for just seven people. Mrs Hobson had murmured coldly that she would see about it. Did madam wish the table to be set with the best china and cutlery?

I had been quite surprised by the question. Aunt Martita would have been ashamed to place anything second-best before a guest, so I said of course Mrs Hobson must use the best of everything. It was only later that I remembered Thorsby was a very different sort of house from Aunt Martita's, and that Mrs Hobson was probably referring to table settings normally reserved for visiting royalty. But it was too late; I would not withdraw my instructions. The housekeeper seemed to swell with pleasure whenever I showed my ignorance or indecision.

On the night of the dinner party, I left Flemynge to dress, and went downstairs early to make sure that everything was as it should be.

The first thing I noticed when I peeped into the dining-room was that nothing at all had been done about the size of the table. Three places were set down one side, two on the other, which meant that the guests would be sitting about five feet apart. Each place setting had an impressive array of cutlery, salts, assorted glasses and huge gold plates. Amazing examples of the gold- and silversmiths' arts were ranged down the centre of the table – a stag hunting scene in silver with little hunters and a stag on a hillside, a chased loving cup, bowls of flowers and four large candelabra. Even the marble-topped side tables were crowded with displays of gold and silver platters as if they were being offered for sale.

In half an hour, when I took my place at the foot of the

table, I would be unable to see Flemynge at the other end, which might be just as well. Inexperience had caused me to order a vulgar display of Thorsby's wealth, creating an atmosphere of formality in which only Flemynge and I would feel completely at sea.

I reached the drawing-room just seconds before Flemynge, Uncle Alfred and Caius entered it. Before I could say anything, the Maltby party was announced. There was no time now to tell Flemynge in which of his dining-rooms we would be eating. I should have done so before, and admitted to myself that my silence had been cowardly.

Introductions were soon made and I knew almost immediately that the evening would be a success. Caius seemed to have been struck dumb by Clarissa's beauty, the Maltbys were at their most ingratiating, and Uncle Alfred was in a jovial mood.

When Grimsby announced that dinner was served, I jumped to my feet, smiling brightly. 'I have a little surprise for everyone. As a way of celebrating Thorsby's return to normal, I have ordered dinner to be served in the large dining-room.'

'Splendid idea!' said Uncle Alfred rather aggressively, as if daring anyone to disagree.

'We are only a small party,' I said, speaking too rapidly, 'but we may pretend we are two dozen.'

When we entered the dining-room, it was Uncle Alfred who set the tone of the evening by commenting on the beauty of the room, saying he felt honoured to be among the first guests to dine in Thorsby since justice had been done. The Maltbys murmured their agreement and the party spread out around the table.

The dining-room did look splendid. The shutters had been closed although it was not quite dark, and the room was bathed in candlelight. The crystal sparkled, the gold flashed. Although three-foot logs, already well alight, hissed and crackled in the fireplace, the room was chilly.

There was a faintly discernible musty smell which airing the room all day had not dispelled. I pulled my shawl more closely round my shoulders, wishing fervently that I didn't have to eat the food which was about to be served.

The tureen of mulligatawny soup was placed at my end of the table, but I would have none of it, so Grimsby filled my soup plate from the other tureen which contained mock turtle soup. No sooner had the tureens been removed than a whole turbot, complete with glassy eye and surrounded by smelts, was placed before me. A faint fishy smell drifted my way and I swallowed hard, feeling hot and cold at the same time.

'The evening is a success,' said Uncle Alfred softly when Sir Hesketh's attention was elsewhere. 'How clever of you to flatter us all with this splendid party.'

'Will the Maltbys think we are vulgar?'

'Never, because you aren't. Having dinner served in here was a masterstroke.' He lowered his voice still further. 'Certain types of persons will need to be reminded of your wealth and station from time to time. You are an unusual person. I suggest you try for a reputation as an eccentric. The Polite World loves eccentrics, especially rich and beautiful ones.'

'I already have a reputation as a madwoman. Is that not eccentric enough?'

Uncle Alfred, for once in his life, looked thoughtful and a trifle sad. 'You are the sanest woman I have ever met and will undoubtedly be the most successful mistress in Thorsby's history. Believe me, I will do whatever I can to help you become established.'

After dinner, when we three women had arranged ourselves comfortably before the fire, Lady Maltby said I must bless myself every day to be living at Thorsby with a handsome, wealthy husband.

'I don't give a fig for Thorsby or for Flemynge's fortune,' I said. 'Nothing matters when . . . I just wish . . . He is so secretive that I don't know –'

'What is he secretive about?'

'If I knew that it wouldn't be a secret! He doesn't tell me what he is thinking.'

'Oh, dear Elinor,' said Lady Maltby earnestly. 'We must not ask our husbands what they are thinking, lest they turn round and ask us the same question.'

'When I asked him, perfectly reasonably, if he intended to leave me at Thorsby and go off on a plant-hunting expedition, all he said was "Don't be absurd". That is no answer.'

'It is an answer of sorts,' said Lady Maltby. 'Forgive me for asking, but are you in the family way?'

'Yes, I am, but it is so early. Does everyone know?'

'I didn't,' said Clarissa.

'I'm sure your secret is safe for several months. I guessed, you see, because you have – I don't know – a look about the eyes. And you ate very little. You know, sometimes women in your condition have strange fancies.'

'I am not having strange fancies. I am justified in my complaint. Flemynge is not being fair. Marriage should be a matter of give and take. I know the Latin names of twenty-five plants and the common names of dozens, while he doesn't know how I mix my colours or the techniques I use. He has never heard of Mr Turner, doesn't want to know about him, and shows no interest at all in the subject of water-colouring. Meanwhile, I have been subjected to more information about Mr Robert Brown than I think entirely necessary.'

'Well . . .' blinked Lady Maltby, at a loss.

'My father doesn't know the first thing about Mama's embroidery,' said Clarissa.

'Is that what you mean?' exclaimed Lady Maltby. 'You want your husband to take an interest in your pastimes? Oh, fatal, I assure you. Keep something of yourself for yourself. And you would be well advised not to attempt to study botany under your husband's guidance. The next thing you know, he will be wishing to take you in hand and insisting that you read *The Times*!'

I smiled in spite of myself. 'He has already done so. But that's not important; I enjoy it, to tell you the truth. No, what I want is something different. I want to have a share in the decisions that have to be made from day to day. When Flemynge found me at Chennings, he made up his mind that I must be rescued and that he would marry me. He ordered some clothes for me, engaged the services of a vicar, bought a special licence, and then one day just came to Chennings and whisked me away. It was all very romantic. I was grateful to have my life settled so easily. But while it is divine to be rescued from dire circumstances by a strong, silent man, one wants a very different sort of person for a husband.'

'I'm so sorry to hear that you are unhappy –' began Lady Maltby.

'I'm not unhappy at all!' I said vehemently. 'Flemynge is the most wonderful man in the world and I'm very happy. Of course I am. I just don't want him to shut me out of his thoughts.'

Lady Maltby reached across to pat my hand. 'Men are by nature imperfect. I think you would rather your husband had his particular set of imperfections than those of most men, and – Why, here are the gentlemen to join us! So soon, too. How good they are.'

I refused to look in Flemynge's direction as he entered the room, but when he passed behind the settee where I was sitting, he first gave my shoulder a quick gentle squeeze, then briefly caressed the back of my neck. I looked up at him quickly, then away as foolish tears filled my eyes, aware that both Lady Maltby and Clarissa had witnessed the fleeting moment. I felt wretched to have been so disloyal.

'Caius has decided to marry,' announced Uncle Alfred, and all eyes swivelled towards the grinning young man. 'Unfortunately, he finds he is short of a suitable bride and somewhere to live, but these are minor difficulties. Now that he has spent a few weeks at Thorsby and observed married bliss at close quarters, he cannot wait to be leg shackled.'

'Father, you do me an injustice,' laughed Caius. 'I have found many suitable brides and cannot choose between them.'

'Yes,' replied his father, fondly. 'Dalliance is your middle name. A suitable home will certainly be the greater problem.'

# Chapter Ten

Uncle Alfred made a very pretty speech the day after the dinner party. I was feeling delicate; he and Caius must not take advantage of our hospitality any longer. They would pack their bags and leave Thorsby the next day. The *three* of us, he said with a broad wink, must visit him at Higgleton Great Hall in the spring. He was just a poor widower, but his daughter-in-law, the wife of his elder son, James, would do the honours.

I gathered later that the daughter-in-law would be 'doing the honours' rather sooner than the spring as the Maltby family were going to stay, because Caius must be given another chance to see the beautiful Clarissa.

We stood on the driveway and waved at Uncle Alfred's coach as it drove away. Caius, a young man whose sweetness and aesthetic sensitivity had greatly impressed me, leaned out of the window and waved affectionately until the coach was out of sight.

'Isn't it strange?' I said to Flemynge. 'Thorsby means different things to different people. It is your inheritance; owning this house puts right an old injustice. Aubrey Presscott wants to own Thorsby because it would confer power and status on him. I hate Thorsby because everyone here thinks I'm mad. Only Caius loves the house for itself. And he loves every piece of furniture, vase and painting.'

'This house is our child's heritage,' said Flemynge.

'A poor heritage to be born among people who will hate him. You and I weren't bred for Thorsby. We are simpler people. Besides, I don't want to be the caretaker of a house of treasures. I want to create a home of my own.'

'I am very sorry that marrying me has made you so unhappy,' said Flemynge and walked off in the direction of Mr Stornaway's office.

I found Mrs Hobson waiting impatiently for me in the hall. 'May I have a word with you, Mrs Flemynge?'

I could think of no reason for refusing. We walked in silence to the morning-room, and because I was feeling excessively tired, I sat down.

'I shall be leaving tomorrow morning,' she said.

'Without giving notice? Am I right in presuming you don't want a letter of recommendation? For you won't get one. I'm flattered, given your obvious opinion of me, that you came to say goodbye.'

'I've not come to ask for a character, nor to say goodbye. I have bought my own establishment with my savings, and will be letting rooms to gentlemen. I've come to tell you what everyone hereabouts thinks of you, but won't say. You and your husband have blighted this house, destroyed for ever its fine character. Joanna Flemynge started the rot, now her bastard son has completed its destruction. Everyone hates you. Thorsby should be burnt to the ground with the two of you in it. That would cleanse the earth.'

'Get out.'

Mrs Hobson was pushing her gloves on to each finger, ramming the leather down hard. 'The wrong you have done to Aubrey Presscott can never be undone, not even if you were to move away from here tomorrow and leave Thorsby to him. Too many lives have been twisted since the bastard took up residence.'

'Mr Aubrey Presscott never had a right to Thorsby any more than his father did. It was always Joanna Flemynge's, entailed to her first born. I know, I've seen the legal documents.'

'There is such a thing as natural justice. Aubrey loved this house and knew how to appreciate it. Now you're here. Pearls before swine. A curse on you and the monster you are carrying.'

Somers was outraged when I told her a few minutes later what Mrs Hobson had said. She insisted that I lie down, and went in search of Flemynge who came to me some minutes later and sat on the side of the bed to take my hand in his.

'She cursed our child,' I said.

'She cannot hurt us and will be gone from this house tomorrow morning. You need not see her again.'

'She cursed our child, Flemynge! I can't forget that. To be so hated... What have I done to her that she would say such a thing to me?'

'Displaced her lover,' said Somers primly. 'Good riddance to bad rubbish, I say. I know someone who would be an excellent housekeeper for Thorsby. With your permission, Mr Flemynge, I could have a word with Mr Stornaway.'

Flemynge urged me to take some laudanum, but I said I would not be drugged. With a worried frown, he stood up and ordered Somers to come with him to discuss the employment of a new housekeeper with Mr Stornaway.

All day I refused to leave my bed, ate very little and could not even concentrate sufficiently to entertain myself by reading. Inevitably, I was wide awake when Flemynge came to bed that night. Only then did I consent to take a few drops of laudanum in a glass of water to help me sleep. Somers was called from her bed to prepare the draught, and Flemynge stood over me to make sure I finished every drop. He seemed very tired; he said he had been in the saddle most of the day touring the estate, and had spent the evening poring over the household accounts.

He slept almost as soon as his head rested on the pillow, while I lay awake, open-eyed in the darkness as I waited for the laudanum to take effect and cast out my morbid thoughts.

Eventually, I did fall asleep and must have slept very deeply. Nevertheless, the sound of shutters banging brought me fully awake with a pounding heart. For several seconds I lay perfectly still, listening. Then I slipped quietly from the bed and let myself out into the hall. The laudanum had made me a little light-headed and gave me a feeling of being slightly removed from my surroundings, but I walked steadily enough and very quietly.

I opened the saloon door and stepped inside, having just enough time to notice that the terrace doors stood open, before someone pounced upon me.

A hand clutched my throat, another stabbed my arm with a sharp instrument. I turned my head in time to receive the second blow on my left ear, a pain that caused me to scream. I tried to push off my attacker, afraid now for my eyes. My assailant continued to stab me. At first, I covered my face with both hands, and took the blows on the backs of them. As the shock of the attack wore off, I became angry, filled with a fury that gave me strength. Frantic now, I clawed with both hands, scratching, turning, screaming as I fought back. Suddenly, I grabbed a handful of hair, long, silky. Lucinda Presscott!

We wrestled in confusion, our voluminous nightgowns hampering our actions. The girl brought me down, straddling me. I rolled over; she fell off but returned to the attack. By the faint light from the hall, I was able to see her shape, see her arm raised repeatedly as she slashed and stabbed, scoring a direct hit sometimes, mostly, thank God, missing her target.

'Kill!' she growled.

Crawling away on my hands and knees, I called to Flemynge, but my arms gave way when Lucinda leapt on my back, still stabbing. I was beyond registering the pain of each individual blow, assumed I must be covered in blood, and kept my head turned away to protect my eyes.

Flemynge rushed into the room, set down his candle and reached for Lucinda. In her hand was a metal nail file, six inches long, a brutal weapon capable of blinding me. Flemynge took her under the arms and tried to lift her off me, but discovered, as I had, that the frail Lucinda had enormous strength tonight. She twisted away from him, to roll down on her back, then up to her feet with the power and fluid speed of a wildcat, ready to stab him if the opportunity arose, not speaking but making grotesque animal noises, growls and yelps among the ragged attempts to catch her breath.

He judged his moment and dived for her hand, the one that held the nail file. She flung her free arm round his neck, closing in, clinging and biting his shoulder, while he concentrated on bending her little finger back until we heard a sickening crack. Grunting, Lucinda dropped the file, but seemed to be unaware of her broken finger as she tried to sink her teeth into his neck.

I lurched across the floor on hands and knees to claw up the nail file and received a kick in the ribs from Lucinda just before Flemynge inadvertently stepped on my hand as he continued to struggle to master the girl.

The kick had thrown Lucinda slightly off balance. Flemynge saw his chance, backed off a pace and dealt the girl a blow, back-handed, starting low on his left side and carrying through as she crashed backwards, falling over me because I was kneeling behind her. Her head cracked against the floorboards and she lay still, the maniacal expression wiped from her demented face, leaving her looking little more than twelve years old and remarkably peaceful.

'Ring for the servants,' said Flemynge, but he was not talking to me. Somers had joined us. She had taken time to put on a dressing-gown before coming downstairs. Her face was white as she tugged the bell-pull before coming with clucks of sympathy to attend to me.

Flemynge reached me first. 'Will you never do as you

are told? I said I didn't want you to come downstairs.'

'You said there was no one down here. I knew I was right. I'm not mad, you see? Lucinda Presscott has visited this room before. Perhaps she has a key. Now you *must* believe me.'

'Ah, Caxton,' said Flemynge to his valet who stood in the doorway looking quite stunned. 'Dash upstairs and fetch my robe and my wife's. Somers, raise the household. Hurry. Elinor, my dear foolish wife, I always thought it possible that Lucinda Presscott had come here exactly as you told it. I didn't wish you to risk your life if it were true. Why will you not leave these things to me? I want to protect you, but you won't allow me to.'

'She hasn't hurt me,' I said, looking down at the unconscious girl. 'I don't mind about my wounds. I cannot tell you what it means to me to be able to prove to everyone that I was right.'

'To be able to prove to yourself that you were right,' corrected Flemynge.

Caxton and Somers returned at about the same time, and Grimsby was not far behind. All at once, my stab wounds began to throb in unison. I was very grateful to Somers for her gentle ministrations, and was properly covered by my dressing-gown and even wearing slippers by the time Mrs Hobson hurried into the saloon.

'Miss Lucinda!' she cried and knelt down beside the girl who was just recovering consciousness. 'What have these beasts done to you? Here, my dear, allow me to help you to stand.'

Lucinda grunted dumbly as Mrs Hobson helped her up.

Grimsby stepped forward and took the girl's arms. 'James has gone to Essex Grange to fetch the girl's brother. I understand Mrs Presscott has gone away to stay with her sister and cannot be fetched immediately. We must tie her up for safety, Mrs Hobson. She has just made a murderous attack on Mrs Flemynge.'

'Tie her up?' cried Mrs Hobson. 'What are you thinking of? This is Miss Lucinda Presscott of Thorsby Hall. She must be treated with respect.'

'She is mad,' said Flemynge quietly, 'and must be treated with compassion, but also, I'm afraid, with caution. Can no one find a robe for her? And a doctor. Elinor, my dear, we must send for the doctor to treat your wounds.'

'No!' I said, putting a hand to my aching ear. 'I don't want to see the doctor. I shall go upstairs when I have caught my breath. Only bed rest will save my baby. I must rest; the doctor can do nothing but tell me to stay as quiet as possible.'

We were a strange sight that night: Flemynge and I seated side by side on one of the magnificent settees while Lucinda lay stretched out on another, trussed hand and foot. A pillow had been placed beneath her head and she was soon decently covered by a blanket fetched from Mrs Hobson's room.

The housekeeper had insisted that a glass of brandy be brought to the girl, but Lucinda refused to drink. She seemed to feel no pain from her broken finger, but Mrs Hobson spoke of little else. Almost every servant in the house was now standing in the saloon or crowding about the doorway from the hall, trying to catch a glimpse of Lucinda and myself. They were unusually silent and, therefore, heard every vituperative word Mrs Hobson said.

Flemynge allowed her to rant on unchecked. He wore a slight frown, and I wondered what he was thinking. I hadn't the energy to ask him. The recent excitement, coupled with the laudanum, had left me very tired. I wanted only to sleep.

About a quarter of an hour later, Aubrey Presscott pushed his way through the press of servants with a few curses to spare and a single angry glance at his sister, whose wild eyes showed no sign of recognition.

'Now, what is this story you have concocted about my sister, Flemynge?'

Flemynge stood up. 'She entered this room wearing nothing but her nightgown. How she entered, I don't know. Perhaps she has a key. My wife heard a noise and came down to investigate. Your sister set upon her with a long nail file. Awakened by a scream, I came downstairs and was forced to knock your sister unconscious in order to save my wife's life.'

'You struck Lucinda? I ought to knock you down.'

'You are welcome to try. Presscott, your sister is demented. She is a danger to herself and others. You must send for a doctor. I am afraid you will have to commit her to an asylum. There are a few which treat their patients with great compassion, allow them a private servant and amusements of all kinds. I will furnish you with the name of one.'

'A Presscott in a madhouse? I think not. Lucinda has been tortured by your presence in her old home. She will recover herself soon. There is nothing wrong with her. Perhaps I should have come here myself and burned the place to the ground. Now I think of it, you are probably lying. It didn't happen as you said.'

'Explain your sister's presence here in her nightgown, if you can. You have no capacity for facing unpleasant truths, Presscott. I know that. Your sister requires urgent attention, yet you have not even spoken to her.'

Aubrey Presscott turned, at last, to his sister. Mrs Hobson was kneeling beside her, moistening her face with a cloth wrung out in witch hazel. He pushed the housekeeper aside and stood over the deranged girl.

'Well, Lucinda, what have you to say about all this?'

Lucinda turned her head away, but Presscott took her by the chin and forced her to look at him.

'Aubrey, consider the poor girl's nerves,' said Mrs Hobson.

'I don't need advice from you, madam,' he said

roughly. 'Barlow! Where is Barlow? There you are, you lazy fellow. Is my groom here? The two of you must carry my sister to the carriage. We are going to the Grange.'

Aubrey Presscott had obviously dressed quickly. His hair was not so carefully combed as usual. He wore neither cravat nor waistcoat and had not even taken the time to put on his shoes. His feet were covered by a scruffy pair of slippers. He had not lost his arrogant, aristocratic air, however. 'You will hear from my lawyer, Flemynge.'

'That may be wise,' said my husband. 'I have been thinking about the arrangement made by your mother. I will honour my side of the bargain. You *mother* may live in the dower house for the rest of her life. Your *sister* may not. I won't have that poor demented girl roaming Thorsby's grounds. She would be a constant threat to my wife, and perhaps to others.'

'My mother may go to the devil for all I care. I will never speak to her again if she moves into the dower house and so I have told her. My mother, sister, even my father – all have failed me. As for Lucinda, no Presscott will ever go to a madhouse.'

Barlow and the groom had removed Lucinda to the carriage. Aubrey Presscott now followed them from the room, the curious servants parting meekly to allow him to pass. I believe every person present that night felt sorry for the young man who had been brought so low in a few short weeks. Every person, that is, except my husband. I glanced at Flemynge and read naked hatred in his face. Hildebrand Presscott had been the cause of so much of Flemynge's unhappiness during his childhood that he couldn't be expected to tolerate the family, especially as the young Presscott was a most unpleasant man.

Not for the first time, I prayed that we might soon move away from Thorsby. For our peace of mind, we ought to live elsewhere. Yet Flemynge had spoken of the dower house and Mrs Presscott in a way that made me think he had no intention of ever leaving Thorsby.

I was very weak, able to stand only with Somers' helping hand. We walked slowly from the room, and the servants parted for us just as they had for Aubrey Presscott. I wondered what they were thinking; there was certainly no clue in their blank faces. Like sheep, they obeyed Flemynge's brusque instructions to return to their beds.

By the time we reached the bedroom, all my wounds were aching fiercely, but miraculously I felt no contractions. Somers counted and treated twenty-five places where the nail file had pierced my skin and added her voice to my husband's when he insisted that I take yet another draught of laudanum. Even this did not allow me an untroubled night. There was no position in which I could comfortably lie, and my tossing and turning kept Flemynge awake until the dawn light began to creep round the edge of the shutters. Then, for some reason, we both slept.

It was late morning when I woke to find Flemynge, fully dressed for riding, sitting on the side of the bed with a letter in his hand.

'Elinor, I would not have awakened you, except that I have received some very good news and must go immediately to London. It seems the Baker family have tired of your estate. My offer was too good for them to ignore. In short, Mr Baker is in London, wishing to complete the sale as quickly as possible.'

'But that's wonderful!'

'I wish it had come at another time. I will have to be away overnight, and frankly, my love, I don't trust you to take care of yourself. I love you very much. Childbirth is extremely dangerous; I must not lose you. Please, beloved, do not take any chances with your health while I am away. Rest as much as possible.'

I reached up to touch his smoothly shaven cheek. 'I

promise you I will not even leave the estate. To tell you the truth, I am too tired to do anything energetic. It is enough to know that you will have the deeds for the Old Manor House in your pocket when you return.'

'We will visit Gloucestershire when you feel well enough, but I can't make any promises about moving from Thorsby. I know you are fond of Caius. It would be a simple matter to rent Thorsby to him and move away. But Thorsby is our child's inheritance, Elinor. His or hers by right. I have a duty to preserve it. I understand your bitter feelings, but consider a moment. One day Caius will marry and have a family of his own. Are we then to have another feud, this time between his eldest and ours?

'I will not walk away from my responsibilities and neither must you. We must find a way to live useful lives. I've been slow to realize what I might do here, but now I know. I shall turn these grounds into a living museum of plants. It seems to me now that my whole life has been in preparation for this work.'

'And what about me?' I asked bitterly. 'What has my life prepared me for?'

'Motherhood, surely. Most women find that raising a family is sufficient fulfilment. But you are also a painter.'

'I don't want to have my life governed by fate. I want to *choose*. Fate took away my parents, fate placed me in the care of my uncle, fate committed me to a madhouse and, yes, fate made me your wife. I love you, Flemynge, truly I do, but I didn't *choose* you. Nor did I decide to have a child, but I have *chosen* to live in Gloucestershire.'

He said nothing for several seconds, long enough for me to wonder if he would take our child from me and send me into Gloucestershire alone. He would certainly be within his legal rights to do so. But all he said was: 'You are distraught. I'm sorry, my dear. We will speak of it later.'

Somers bustled into my room the following morning and could scarcely bring herself to open the shutters before telling me her great news.

Barlow was seated this very minute in the servants' hall, had come to beg a bed for the night. Might he not sleep in the attic, just until he found another position, she asked. Everything was at sixes-and-sevens, what with Mrs Hobson leaving, and all. Such a to-do!

'What has happened?' I asked, sitting up in bed. 'Why was Barlow dismissed?'

'They all were, ma'am, all the servants except Mister Aubrey's groom, that dirty old man, Foxley. Mister Aubrey's closing the house down immediately. A doctor is expected from London to see Miss Lucinda, and Mister Aubrey was in such a hurry to get rid of everyone that there isn't even a female in the house to attend her!'

The maid came over to hand me a shawl for my shoulders. 'Oh, I almost forgot. That bank! Presscott and Stracey. It's been closed and some of the partners arrested for fraud. No one knows what will happen to Mister Aubrey.'

'Oh, Somers, how sad! One must feel sorry for them all.'

Somers didn't share my view. The Presscotts had been overbearing and disagreeable to their servants for many years. There was no pity for them below stairs now that they had fallen so low.

My many little wounds no longer troubled me greatly except for the scratch across my face and the several places on the backs of my hands which hurt every time I flexed my fingers. Somers was soothing about my disfigured face, anxious to assure me that I would not be permanently scarred.

To tell the truth, I was not particularly worried about my appearance. I had other problems on my mind. I had been so certain that if I could prove that Lucinda Presscott was mad, all my troubles would cease and I would be able to face the future contentedly.

By good fortune, I had proved that she was mad, and that I was not. Yet, I could take no pleasure in the knowledge. One struggle was over. Now I had to fight another battle to be allowed to move from Thorsby. And I knew in my heart that I would lose the struggle this time.

The news that Somers brought me depressed me greatly. The assorted misfortunes of the Presscott family weighed down my spirits, especially knowing that young Lucinda might spend the rest of her life in a madhouse. I could not bear to think of that. Mrs Presscott had appeared to me as a proud, hard woman, incapable of finer feelings. How would she react to the loss of her home and husband, the incarceration of her daughter and the possible arrest of her son? Even pride and insensitivity could not shield her from intolerable pain, I thought.

There was no point in trying to explain my sombre mood to Somers. I ate breakfast in my room, put on a simple wool gown, half boots and a thick woollen shawl. Then, refusing Somers' offer to accompany me as she sometimes did, I went outdoors for my daily walk in the grounds.

Autumn was well and truly upon us. The sky was overcast; every sudden gust of wind brought another flurry of yellow leaves floating to the ground, and there was a definite sting in the air. My hands ached and I wished I had worn gloves.

The graceful stone bridge drew me. I walked down the hill and stood gazing at the stream. I had tried to commit the bridge to paper many times, but bricks and mortar always defeated me. On many occasions my long-suffering art master had tried to instruct me in the mysteries of perspective, but I could not learn. I succeeded more often with plants and landscapes. Flemynge's lectures on botany, which I once hated, had taught me more that was of value to me as a painter than

I had ever admitted to him. Understanding all about the various parts of plants enabled me to draw flowers with greater feeling as well as accuracy. As a result, my flower paintings gave me satisfaction whereas my other efforts so often left me feeling frustrated.

Perhaps if I made a similar effort to know about Thorsby's contents, the home farm and the other properties, I might learn to tolerate the house. This novel idea came to me in a flash of understanding, but there was no time to pursue the thought.

A man emerged from the trees and with some surprise I watched him approach. I recognized him as Aubrey Presscott's groom and asked him sharply what he was doing on Thorsby's grounds.

'Message from Mrs Presscott, ma'am,' he said, looking round him anxiously. 'She asked me to find a way of speaking to you in private like. She is waiting in the dower house, Mrs Flemynge, and would like a word with you without the whole of Thorsby knowing about it.'

'She must be very distressed about her daughter.'

The groom looked down. 'Yes'm. Will you walk kind of casual like over to the dower house now? I'll go out the door in the wall over there like I come in.'

I felt the least I could do would be to speak kindly to Mrs Presscott, perhaps to explain to her what sort of treatment she could expect to obtain for her daughter. I wished now that I had asked which madhouse Flemynge had in mind when he told Aubrey Presscott he could recommend one. Certainly, the Quakers treated only their own and would not accept Lucinda.

I expected to find Mrs Presscott standing outside the dower house. I had locked it after I left her on the last occasion and didn't have a key with me now. But I could see from several yards away that the front door was standing ajar. So the Presscotts had a key! And probably others to various doors at Thorsby. I would ask Mrs

Presscott about it and make sure that all keys were returned to me.

I pushed the door open and stepped inside the gloomy hall. The door shut behind me with a bang and I turned to see Aubrey Presscott locking it.

'Mr Presscott, there is nothing –'

'I know. You expected to see my mother. You would prefer not to see any of us. You wish we would go away so that you might forget all about us. I understand, believe me, I do. That is why Foxley lied to you. I knew you wouldn't come at my request and knew, too, that you would not miss an opportunity to gloat over my mother's many tragedies. You have all you ever desired, a change of fortune that must surely take your breath away every time you think of it. Can't you spare a few minutes for a man who has lost everything he valued?'

He had succeeded in making me feel churlish, so I reluctantly agreed to listen to him, although I was uneasy. No one knew I was in the dower house, and the man had locked us in.

I moved over to the door as casually as I could, and leant my back against it with my hands behind me. My fingers closed on the key, but Mr Presscott seemed unaware of it.

'You would not be living at Thorsby today if my father had kept his nerve and refused to move away,' he said, and I nodded. Lawyers are notorious for keeping legal matters, especially those connected with inheritances, going for ever. Flemynge would have had to call on his uncle's wealth to help him press his claim, and even then could not have been sure of the outcome.

'Then,' continued Mr Presscott, 'Flemynge brought you to the Grange, choosing to introduce you to us in the most provocative way. My sister never recovered from the shock of seeing you as you were that day. Wasn't that a despicable trick? Do you not wonder about your husband's curious need for revenge? Do you not deplore his ruthlessness?'

'My husband heard nothing at his mother's knee but the need for revenge. I don't blame him for the action which, incidentally, he later regretted.' I sighed, pulling my shawl more closely round my shoulders. I had turned the key while talking and felt confident of leaving whenever I chose. 'Why can you and my husband not realize that you have no quarrel with one another? Your father and my mother-in-law were the mischief makers.'

'No quarrel! Flemynge has taken my home from me.'

'Admit the truth, Mr Presscott. Your father stole Thorsby. Had he not done so, you would have been able to adjust to a different way of life long ago.'

'Joanna Flemynge was a hellcat and a whore, my father a mean-minded simpleton. But their quarrel has descended to Flemynge and me. It is our destiny to carry on the battle.'

'Oh, what piffle! If you believe that, why have you come to talk to me? I have nothing further to say, except that your mother will be able to take up residence in the dower house whenever she wishes.' I turned to open the door.

Presscott shouted: 'Now!'

The door flew open in my face, knocking me back into Aubrey Presscott's arms as the groom rushed in. Between them they had no difficulty in tying my hands behind me and binding my feet together. I screamed and struggled and begged them to release me, but my terror seemed to bring them pleasure. The harder I struggled, the more brutally they handled me.

A closed carriage was standing on the driveway about fifteen yards from the dower house. I was tossed inside like a sack of flour and Aubrey Presscott leapt in beside me to jerk me by the arm into a sitting position. The groom mounted the box and urged the horse into a trot.

'You promised, guvnor!' shouted Foxley over his shoulder. 'You said you wouldn't hurt her.'

'And I meant it,' said my captor, leering at me. 'I will not hurt you, dear Mrs Flemynge. You are safe from me. Incidentally, you will also be safe from your husband's loving attentions. For eternity. Don't you think that is rather clever of me?'

# Chapter Eleven

I felt as if the breath had been squeezed out of me, but managed to whisper: 'Where are you taking me?'

'Where you will never be found, of course. Oh, Mrs Flemynge! How can I express my gratitude to you for providing me with the perfect revenge against your husband? He deserves to be punished. God *wants* me to punish him.'

'How can you say such a blasphemous thing? Foxley! Don't be a party to this wickedness! Turn back!'

Foxley laughed. 'I'm not risking my neck, ma'am. Nobody's going to arrest old Foxley for nothing.'

'Foxley has seen the will of God operating in these past moments,' said Presscott. 'You see, we never expected you to be waiting for him on the bridge. We knew that you were in the habit of walking in the grounds each day and that a visit to the bridge was a part of your tour. That much Hobson told me some weeks ago. But Foxley and I expected to have to wait for hours! You usually don't come out so early. You gave me quite a turn arriving, as you did, scarcely twenty minutes after I had entered the dower house. In fact, I thought for a moment that it might be someone else. And then there you were! God's will.'

'You will hang for this, Mr Presscott. You will be found out and you will hang for having abducted me.'

'Oh, no, I will never be found out. My plan is foolproof, so perfect that I can't resist telling you about it.'

'Beware, Master Aubrey!' called Foxley. 'Don't tell her nothing.'

'No, no, I really must speak of it. I want Mrs

Flemynge to appreciate the joke. You see, it all has to do with my sister, Lucinda. Poor dear, she was not at all herself after I fetched her home from Thorsby. As your husband advised, I was forced to call in a doctor to examine her. But I was too sly to send for that fool, Mackintosh, in the village. Oh no, I sent to London for a doctor. A gentleman known to me only by name. He had done me a great service, for a fee, several years ago when a lady friend found herself carrying an unwanted burden.'

'Your sister deserves the finest medical attention. How could you allow an abortionist to examine her?'

'There was very little examining to be done. He asked her a few questions to which she made no intelligible reply. He was, therefore, prepared to sign the committal notice he had brought with him. The doctor showed considerable foresight; it was already signed by a magistrate.'

'You must send her to a proper institution, not a dreadful place like Chennings.'

Aubrey Presscott began to laugh. He laughed so loudly and for so long that for several seconds he couldn't speak. He removed a handkerchief from his sleeve and wiped his eyes, took several deep breaths and battled with a ferocious attack of hiccups before he was finally able to continue.

'You may be sure I will not send Lucinda to Chennings. Pay attention. What I am going to tell you next is the most important part of my scheme. The doctor said he would sign the committal form straight away, but I told him that no Presscott would ever be sent to a madhouse. "Well then," said the doctor. "I'll put a false name on the document." '

I felt my heart begin to pound furiously. 'What name did he write?' I whispered.

'Can't you guess? How surprising! You seem to be such a quick-witted female. He wrote – on my instructions – the name Elinor Flemynge.'

'You intend to commit your sister to a madhouse in my name?'

'Of course not! I'm going to commit Fitzroy Flemynge's wife to a madhouse in her own name. What is more, I am going to commit Elinor Flemynge to Chennings. No one will think of looking for you there.'

For a moment, I was blinded by an enveloping red glow of terror, but, strangely, this feeling quickly faded to be replaced by a sensation I can only describe as euphoria. For weeks, memories of Chennings and the fear of returning there had been my waking and sleeping nightmare. My fear had crowded out all other emotions so that I was unable to love Flemynge freely or to rejoice in the child I was carrying. Now, by a bizarre twist of fate, I was about to confront my fear and lay the ghost of Chennings for ever.

I never doubted for a moment that Mr McCann would refuse to take me in. He knew Flemynge was a magistrate, knew that I was sane. He would not risk trouble with the law. Aubrey Presscott, by delivering me to Chennings, would ensure that I was handed over to the one man who could be depended upon to contact Flemynge.

Letting out my breath in a long sigh, I slumped against the corner of the carriage and closed my eyes. The two men laughed delightedly at my apparent defeat. Meanwhile, I concentrated on hiding my relief, my anticipation of triumph. The horse was tiring; our pace slowed considerably. No one spoke for some time, until Foxley called: 'There it is!'

I opened my eyes as we entered through the gateway of Chennings.

'Rather a grim structure, don't you think?' asked Presscott cheerfully. 'I'm sure you will live a long unhappy life here.'

Mr and Mrs McCann were both standing in the drive by the time our coach stopped and I had been dragged out. Leaving me in the strong hands of Foxley, Presscott swaggered over to the waiting couple.

'Good day to you. What is your name?'

'McCann, sir, and this is my wife.' Mrs McCann sketched an awkward curtsey. She and her husband made a strong contrast to the splendidly dressed Presscott. Their clothes were faded and patched. Mrs McCann seemed to have lost a great deal of weight and consequently looked older than I remembered her.

'Well, McCann, I have brought you a patient.'

'*Her?*'

'My cousin, Fitzroy Flemynge, is, as you know, a magistrate. I'm sorry to say he took advantage of his powers to remove this woman from Chennings a few months ago. To spite his family, he even married her. The action served its purpose; he has wrested a great deal of money from his relatives and now has no further use for the wench.'

'I don't know . . .' began McCann.

'You see this paper? It bears the name Elinor Flemynge and is signed by a doctor and a magistrate. The woman has been properly certified insane.'

'Just as I always thought,' murmured Mrs McCann, and I shouted 'No!'

'This is not a philanthropic institution. I know that, old fellow.' Presscott held up a fat purse. 'Therefore, will one hundred guineas, paid in advance, be suitable? I shall send another payment of equal size in six months' time if the female is still alive. I am going abroad today, but will return in a few months.'

'It's a lie!' I struggled in Foxley's grip, but he was a strong man, although no taller than I.

'Clean off her head,' said Foxley as the McCanns continued to look doubtful.

'Very well then.' McCann slipped the purse of coins into his coat pocket. 'If your man will bring her indoors, I'll lock her in a bedchamber until I can treat her.'

Foxley dragged me forward, although I resisted every step of the way. 'I'm not insane! My husband will come for me! I am expecting a child!'

McCann paused, looked up at Presscott greedily as he held out his hand. Aubrey Presscott smiled at me, then dropped another few guineas in the upheld palm. 'Amusing, isn't it, Mrs Flemynge, that your *treatment* at Chennings is being paid for by the sale of one of Thorsby's most exquisite miniatures? Fortunately, I had sold it before my mother misguidedly returned Thorsby's contents.'

He turned to McCann. 'It would be a tragedy if a madwoman should give birth to an infant lunatic, wouldn't it?'

'Oh, if the child is born alive, it will be put out for adoption, sir,' said Mrs McCann.

I screamed as they all joined in the struggle to drag me through the small parlour, down a passageway to my old cell. It was so dark here that the four of them were stumbling over each other as well as over me. But they managed the business fairly quickly. I was locked in the cell. They left, all talking at once, and their voices were soon so faint that I could not make out one word in ten.

I was too nauseous and exhausted to do anything but lie down on the filthy bed. Within seconds I had taken the only escape route open to me. I slept. I believe it was many hours later that I was awakened by noises in the adjoining cell. Sitting up in the narrow bed, I knocked on the wall.

'Miss Watson, is that you? It's Elinor Flemynge, that is, Elinor Burns-Roberts.'

'Good heavens!' I heard faintly through the wall, then almost at once Miss Watson's face appeared at the grille of my door, lit by a candle. 'I have a key, my dear. I'm sure it fits your door as well as my own. I lock myself in these days in case Mr McCann . . .'

'You've changed,' I said as Miss Watson put the

candle holder with its fitfully burning candle end on the small table. 'You are well, I can see it in your face.'

'Yes, I am well.' She kissed my cheek. 'I awoke one morning knowing that I wanted to live. Life is good and can be worth while even at Chennings. Or perhaps especially at Chennings. I have won a number of privileges from the McCanns. My loving family are in no hurry to have me back, and the McCanns need the money badly. I have learned to endure. Tell me what has happened to you since I saw you last.'

I told my story as economically as I could, anxious not to waste time. 'So, you see, my husband has no idea where I am,' I finished. 'And will not even know I am missing until tomorrow around midday. I fought the McCanns all the way. Did you not hear my screams?'

'I knew that they had a new patient, but never dreamt it was you. Yes, it's true. You have recovered. You aren't –'

'*Recovered!* There was never anything wrong with me! I was always perfectly sane!'

'My dear . . .' Miss Watson shrugged. 'You must bear your imprisonment as best you can and pray that your husband finds you eventually. The McCanns have fallen on very hard times. The house was full at one time, shortly after you left. Then the sweating sickness broke out among the patients. Megs and Mrs Huckle died, as did all the men. Poor Mrs Porter was very ill, but she pulled through. The McCanns needed my help in nursing the patients, and, of course, their income dwindled as each poor soul died. There are just Mrs Porter and myself and two men, both dangerous.'

She sat down beside me on the bed. 'Parishes have not been eager to send anyone else here, so you can see how they must have been overjoyed to receive a hundred or more guineas for you. But for that very reason, I believe we can persuade the McCanns to treat you as a guest rather than a lunatic. Mrs Porter and I take our meals with them now, and I'm sure you can do the same.'

I was gripping my hands tightly together. 'In so far as I have been obsessed with my own emotions, my own inner thoughts during these past weeks, I grant you that I have not been very healthy mentally. But that is quite a different thing from being insane. To want to survive is normal, Miss Watson. To want freedom is normal. The shock of returning to this place has cleared my mind. You might say it has cured me of selfish introspection. I must protect my child and I must not give my dear husband one moment's worry more than is absolutely necessary. I have learned to think of someone besides myself and that someone will be *demented* when he discovers I have disappeared. So, you see, I have no choice. Whatever the dangers or hardship in walking back to Thorsby, it is preferable to risking the happiness, the very existence of those I love. I promise you, Flemynge and I will come for you, and for Mrs Porter, too, when we can.'

'Forgive me for saying it, Elinor, but to attempt to escape from here is madness. Try to control your impulsive nature. Do not always fight circumstances. Wait patiently. He will come. Surely now, you are mature enough to endure with fortitude.'

'No, that is not my way. I can see you have found your own salvation, your own way of preserving your sanity. Had you not been prepared to accept your imprisonment and to help the McCanns, you might have been truly mad by now. But I'm different. If you don't care for the idea of my walking alone to Thorsby, come with me. We will go together.'

'I can't leave. There are . . . I have responsibilities here. Mrs Porter is one. She is not mad, unless an intense desire for a home and children of one's own is madness. She must be protected from her own excessively friendly nature, of course. Poor thing, she is not very bright. I can't leave her, and she is at this moment locked in the attic.'

She sighed. 'How can I explain to you? The tree that bends weathers the storm, Elinor. It may surprise you to learn that I have become very interested in the treatment of the insane. If it were possible, I would open a madhouse of my own, run on principles laid down by a Quaker family I have read about.'

'The Tukes follow me everywhere,' I said wryly.

At that moment, the tiny candle-end sputtered and went out. We were enveloped in darkness.

'That settles it. I am going now. You are very strong, Miss Watson. I envy you. Are you still holding the key? Go back to your room and forget about me. Tomorrow, tell them you heard nothing.'

We embraced briefly; I waited, seated on the bed, until I heard the key turn in Miss Watson's lock. Standing up, I took a deep breath and attempted to get my bearings. I could feel the bed against the side of my leg. Two strides took me to the door which was standing open. I miscalculated slightly and hit the edge with my right shoulder which made me gasp.

'Take care,' hissed Miss Watson.

I said I would, as I felt the corridor wall with one hand while clutching my shawl tightly closed with the other. Down two steps, I remembered, then two paces and up three more uneven stone steps to the kitchen. No curtains here; I walked through fairly confidently. A half moon in a clear sky meant that I wasn't walking in total darkness. My hand went unerringly to the handle of the parlour door and I let myself in with extreme caution.

The room was small and contained almost all the furniture the McCanns possessed. A settle, loose rugs, a dining table and four chairs, one or two footstools and an old Welsh dresser. It must be very late; there was not even the faintest glow among the ashes in the fireplace to help me get my bearings. The door was in the same wall as the window, I remembered with a sigh of relief.

Although the small casement window had floral curtains, they had not been drawn.

The moon shone brightly, but on my right whereas I thought it should be on my left. I reasoned that I must have turned somewhere along the way, but felt certain of knowing which way to walk towards Thorsby once I was out in the open. Eager now to be gone, I walked boldly in the direction of the window and crashed against something low, perhaps a joint-stool. Instinctively, I flung my hands out and my shawl slid to the ground as my hands made contact not with the window, but with its image in the looking glass. I could make out my own dark shape in it, and over my shoulder, the mocking reflection of the moon.

Nothing for it. I must not panic, but bend to pick up the shawl, then turn right round and head for the window and the door. I had no idea what traps, in the form of low furniture, lay in store for me. Somewhere in the distance, a dog howled. I remembered that the McCanns housed a vicious brute in an outbuilding. Fearfully, I felt for the two bolts on the door, released them as quietly as I could, and walked outside. It was bitterly cold, a possibility I had not taken into consideration. The sharp air made me gasp. It was going to be a long cold walk before the sun rose, and even longer before the day warmed up. The grass was frosty and crisp underfoot. I dared not walk down the middle of the drive, but keeping to the poorly-tended, over-grown grounds would ensure that not only my shoes but also the hem of my gown were soaking wet within minutes. The dog began to bark frantically.

I was almost halfway to the gates of Chennings when a glance over my shoulder showed me that someone had lit a candle in the room directly above the parlour. A shadowy figure darkened the curtain which was almost instantly twitched aside. Mr McCann! Fortunately, I was hidden by some shrubs. He wouldn't see me from his window. Would he be satisfied or would he come outside to look round? The candlelight disappeared from the bedroom. I saw it again at a hall window and didn't wait to find out where it would show itself next. The dog had stopped barking. I lifted my skirts and began to run.

Once outside the gates, which were not locked, I believed I must turn left. The road was narrow and muddy. I had never passed this way in full command of my senses, but thought it continued this way for half a mile before meeting a larger road with a better surface. Cold air lacerated my throat and lungs as I ran. I wouldn't be able to keep up this pace for long, but perhaps I could make it to the main road before stopping for breath. In the distance, I heard the dog begin barking again, followed by the sort of yelps the animal always gave when his master was drawing near. Then silence: McCann putting on the collar, taking up the chain, leaning his weight against the dog's as the beast strained to sniff me out.

A pain was growing in my side; the muscles in my belly tightened, contracting. This couldn't go on, and I was tiring too fast to be able to think clearly about what to do when I stopped running. I had very little idea of a dog's tracking capabilities, but assumed they must be awesome since men set them to tracking foxes and other game.

Within five minutes, McCann had me cornered between a high brick wall and a large dead tree. The dog yelped frantically, anxious to leap at my throat. McCann was furious and roared abuse all the way back to Chennings.

Mrs McCann was waiting for us when we reached the parlour. The lamp was lit and I had the chance to glimpse my own wan face in the mirror before I met Katherine Watson's sad eyes.

'You know what you'll get, don't you?' said McCann shaking me by the arm. 'Here, woman, guard her well whilst I put Bumper back in his kennel. Then I want a word with both of these women.'

Mrs McCann had other ideas. She took me back to my cell straight away and locked the door.

'You can spend the rest of the night thinking about what's going to happen to you,' she said through the grille. 'We were prepared to make things easy for you. Now you've gone and spoiled it. Did you think we would let you go running round the countryside telling tales about us? And you can think about something else, Mrs Flemynge, if that's your name, which I doubt. Think what you've done to Katherine Watson who'll be punished for helping you. She had a very cosy life here until you came back. She will be sorry she ever took pity on you.'

'It wasn't her fault,' I said faintly. 'Please don't hurt her.' But Mrs McCann and the light were gone. I lay on the bed for several minutes taking deep breaths, trying to calculate the time between contractions. Mercifully, they grew weaker and finally stopped altogether. Eventually, I slept until Mrs McCann roused me the next morning and took me to the kitchen for breakfast. I was ravenous but was given nothing but bread and milk while the McCanns smacked their lips over ham and eggs.

Katherine Watson and Mrs Porter were both allowed the freedom to eat their porridge in the kitchen. Indeed, Miss Watson was forced to cook it and serve some to the two male patients before she could have her own. When she returned and took her place at the table, the McCanns were deep in a blood-curdling discussion about cupping and emetics.

'I must remind you, Mr McCann,' said Miss Watson, 'that Mrs Flemynge is expecting a child. If you would have murder on your hands, then by all means indulge in blood letting and pills. However, I warn you, it could be dangerous. Her husband could charge you with murder.'

'And I must tell you, miss, that I don't think her husband will ever come for her. He don't want her.

Probably decided to get rid of her when he found out she was in the family way. What's more, I can hardly write to her aunt and say I allowed her out and she's got herself in calf, now can I? I'll do what I want and you can't stop me.'

Mrs Porter had stopped eating and was now listening to the conversation with her spoon halfway to her mouth. I prayed that for once the girl would remain silent, as Miss Watson continued to argue with McCann.

'You have got yourself in a fine pickle. You have taken in a woman who was abducted from her own garden. Mr Flemynge is a magistrate who loves his wife dearly. Write to him, tell him that his wife is here, that you rescued her from his enemy and will keep her safe until he can come for her. He will reward you for your kindness, I assure you. Why keep her when you can be paid twice without the necessity of giving her more than two meals?'

'What do you think, Charlie?' asked Mrs McCann doubtfully.

'And if he don't want her?'

'You will have lost nothing,' said Katherine Watson, but I could see at once that her argument had failed.

'She was wrongly taken from this place. She's been brought back with all the proper papers. I shall treat her for her condition, and I shall do so every time either you or her or this simpleton here,' he indicated the gaping girl, 'step out of line. So get up and do your chores, the pair of you.'

McCann grinned at me as he shovelled another piece of ham into his mouth. 'So you got yourself in the family way, strumpet. My, my, that was careless of you. Still, I expect I can do something about that. You'll lose it soon enough when you've been cupped and had a few doses of digitalis.'

'You mustn't do that, Mr McCann.' It was what I had been dreading most of all. 'That would be murder.'

'In my capacity as owner of this establishment, I'll do

what I think best, and we'll have no talk of murder if you please. However, I shan't dose you straight away. Since you left, I have been in receipt of a superior method of restoring the wits of lunatics. I got myself a book written by a Quaker up north who has been making a terrible fuss, but he's wrong. Everyone knows that Quakers don't have lunatics the way other folks do. I daresay he never really had a serious case to deal with. He's a menace, I say, and miss smarty boots Watson can say what she likes in his defence. Dosing and cupping *do* help. Why, otherwise, I wouldn't be able to cope with those two brutes we got chained up!'

He took me by the arm, lifted me from my seat and pushed me inexorably along. 'First, I shall try my new method. Then, if you don't come to heel, you'll get all the dosing you can stand.'

Mrs McCann joined us, holding a lantern as we moved towards the cellar door.

The strength had gone from my legs. I thought I would fall down the cellar steps unless McCann's bruising fingers continued to bite into my arm. 'What are you going to do to me down there?'

The stairs were narrow and uneven, the air chilly, damp and filled with coal dust and the stink of the privy refuse. I saw it straight away, a great wooden thing squatting malevolently in the middle of the cellar.

'What is it?' I asked.

'That's the contraption,' laughed McCann, 'that's going to turn you into a model patient. Or else.'

I closed my eyes briefly, praying for strength. No more running; no more defiance. I was left with no alternative but to endure with fortitude what was to come, as Miss Watson had advised. With no idea of how long the torture would last or what its effect would be upon me, I walked forward.

'Not so fast, strumpet. First we must put you in the strait-waistcoat.'

# Chapter Twelve

Mrs McCann brought forward the heavy canvas coat with its long sleeves. I held out my arms so that they could put it on me without a struggle. As they fastened the tabs at the back, I breathed deeply, controlling my panic; a small victory but an important one, victory over a fear that was neither foolish nor irrational. I had discovered the secret of behaving with dignity when others were determined to destroy my self-respect.

Since I was last at Chennings, they had purchased the wooden structure that Mr McCann called the Whirling Chair. It looked like a fairground ride for one person; a stout base supporting a timber that held a chair at its free end. The wood had been sanded to satin, stained and varnished to the highest standards; a machine devised by a fiend and made by a master craftsman. I was quickly strapped into the chair and Mr McCann gave me a hefty push so that I whirled round in a circle no more than nine or ten feet in diameter. The sensation was not particularly unpleasant, and had I stopped after one circuit, I might have said it was a harmless contraption.

I did not stop after the first circuit, however, and by the twentieth I was feeling very sick. Both Mr and Mrs McCann were perspiring as they pushed me round and round. I heard Mrs McCann grunt with the effort to increase my speed whenever it was her turn to push. Soon it was impossible to focus my eyes on anything. The pillars supporting the roof above, the rank air, all the physical manifestations of my imprisonment seemed increasingly unreal as the blood began to pound in my temples.

Freed, as it were, from all earthly things, I achieved a kind of floating sensation and began to think quite clearly and dispassionately. The chair was a devilish invention, but I didn't find it frightening at all. Of course, I was not insane. How terrifying this experience would be for someone who had already lost his reason! The stupidity of using an instrument like the whirling chair to cure madness should be evident to everyone, yet Mr Tuke had written of far worse outrages perpetrated on the helpless insane. Was it not possible that people like the McCanns were more in need of being locked up than those they had in their power?

Remembering my terror last January on discovering I had been put in a madhouse, I began to wonder why I had kept my sanity in this place for many long months, only to find my health declining once I was safely within the boundaries of Thorsby. It seemed that the fear of returning to Chennings was worse than actually living here.

I had reason to congratulate myself on one small point. In the end, despite my increasing melancholia, my withdrawal from Flemynge's love and my total preoccupation with my tumultuous emotions, I had not been forced to return to a madhouse because I was insane, but simply because an enemy of my husband's chose this method to gain his revenge. On the first occasion, I had been afraid that I would never escape: that fear no longer tormented me. I knew Flemynge would move heaven and earth to discover my whereabouts: that was the nature of the man. My trust in his resourcefulness and steadfast love was absolute. My patience might be sorely tried in the coming weeks or months, but he *would* come.

After twenty-five, I lost count of the revolutions. Mrs McCann announced that she was exhausted. I saw her flop into a straight chair and wipe her forehead with the back of her arm. I also saw Mrs Porter, with the tears flowing unchecked down her cheeks, and Katherine Watson, pale and indecisive, as the two of them tried to hide themselves behind a pillar. I wanted to tell them not to worry, that my ordeal was less than it appeared to be, but the dizziness and nausea were so great that I dare not unclench my teeth to speak. Another revolution or two and only Mrs Porter remained. Katherine Watson had left the cellar.

The ringing in my ears had become so loud that the sound of voices reached me as from a great distance. It seemed as if I *saw* Mrs McCann start up from her seat with her mouth open a split second before I heard her scream. Then a confusion of noise, a fleeting glimpse of my husband coming towards me with Miss Watson a few steps behind him. A second later, I and my chair careered into Mr McCann's back as he unthinkingly stood in my inevitable path. I came to a juddering halt that snapped my neck back and sent stars of pain fizzing before my eyes.

Mr McCann, startled by Flemynge's arrival, was caught unawares and fell forward. Flemynge hauled him to his feet by his coat lapels and then knocked him to the ground again with a fist in the face that made McCann's nose bleed. Mrs McCann, screaming still, rushed to her husband's aid as Miss Watson and Mrs Porter set about untying the straps of the chair and loosening the tabs of the strait-waistcoat.

My husband looked older and extremely tired, his usually calm expression twisted into an ugly mask of hate. He shook Mrs McCann's clawing fingers from his coat and hit the whimpering apothecary once again.

'Flemynge, stop it! I am unhurt!' It was true. It was also true that my trembling knees made it impossible for me to stand unaided.

Flemynge left McCann sprawled on the floor and took me from Katherine's supporting hands to hold me in a bone-crushing embrace. I clung to him, revelling in his kisses, dizzy now with relief and the *feel* of him: the stubble on his chin, the hard texture of his woollen jacket. As usual, he had removed his cravat and unfastened the top buttons of his shirt. I kissed the hollow of his neck where a few chest hairs curled, dark and masculine. For the first time, I was able to give myself wholeheartedly, to express my love. Neither of us cared at all if we were providing an embarrassing spectacle for our small audience.

'I thought I would go mad with worry during these last hours,' said Flemynge. 'I'm sure I looked like a madman when Miss Watson opened the door to me.'

'While I, on the other hand, have become sane. Don't look so distressed and don't, please, try to stop me from saying what must be said. I have been given a rare gift: a second chance, the opportunity to return to the scene of a personal defeat and relive the event. This time I faced my ordeal as I wish I had done in January. I have proved the soundness of my mind, and a greater steadiness in my character. Strange as this may seem to you, I would not have missed the experience, although I might think differently if I had been forced to stay here for years.'

'You were never insane, Elinor. How can I convince you of that?'

'No, I was not insane when I was an inmate of Chennings, but later I lost my way. I was obsessed, haunted by this old house and what it represented. In the past hours, I have laid the ghost of Chennings. It's true, my nerves are still sadly stretched. I have recovered enough to be able to admit it. I have not yet completely overcome the melancholy of the past weeks, but with your help I shall get better. Now tell me. How did you find me so quickly?'

'The alarm was raised before I reached Thorsby. Poor Lucinda Presscott was found dead by Barlow who had returned to the Grange to collect a few of his possessions. The doctor in the village said she had been poisoned. By this time, Somers knew that you were nowhere on the estate and Presscott was missing. I doubt if he will ever be found. It was not a great leap of the imagination to guess that Presscott had abducted you. Not surprisingly, no one had any idea where he might have gone. By the time I reached Thorsby, all the servants, in fact the entire village, was convinced that he had murdered you, as well as his sister. I was afraid for your life, but guessed that he might have some other ordeal planned. His mind and mine run along the same lines, I'm afraid. We both like our gestures of revenge to have something of the fiendishly logical about them.'

I tightened my arms around his neck. 'You are not to compare yourself with that man.'

'I must, my dear. When I first confronted Hildebrand Presscott, I told him I would marry and raise a family at Thorsby. I said it to taunt him, nothing more. I had no plans for marriage. Presscott said a woman would have to be mad to marry me. I had not met you then, but I suppose your fate was sealed from that moment. I have been a confused and bitter man; my mother's legacy. I actually thought it would punish Hildebrand Presscott if I installed a madwoman at Thorsby. I have acted in a way that disgusts me every time I think of it. Taking you from Chennings for the reason I did was very wrong. I don't deserve to be rewarded with your sweet love as I have been.'

'You thought I might be just a trifle deranged, didn't you? Please tell me the truth, Flemynge. It's important.'

'Yes, I was doubtful about your sanity in the early days. That is why I went to see Samuel Tuke. Curiously, the moment he said you were insane, I became convinced that you weren't. Nevertheless, I was cautious in my treatment of you, looking for signs of madness. Later, I saw how your nerves were being lacerated by memories of your ordeal and the attitudes of others towards you. I tried to make amends, but quite frankly I didn't know what to do for the best.'

Mr McCann was now seated in the only chair the cellar possessed while his wife dabbed his bleeding face with her apron. 'You had no right to hit me, sir. I have proper documents for this patient, made out in the name of Elinor Flemynge. I was within my rights to try to cure her of her madness by this or any other method. If she is perfectly sane, well then, I am very glad of it, but sometimes it is hard to tell. The document is signed by a doctor, after all.'

I quickly explained to Flemynge how Presscott had contrived to obtain a committal order with my name on it, and told Flemynge that Mr McCann could not be blamed for what he did. 'After all, we both know that worse things are done to helpless people in the name of curing them of their malady. By the way, whatever the McCanns might think, Mrs Porter and Miss Watson are perfectly sane. Neither belongs in a madhouse. They depend upon us to see that justice is done and that they are freed to lead useful lives.'

'We will starve if you take away our patients!' cried Mrs McCann, now wiping her own face with her bloodied apron.

'Mr Flemynge,' said Katherine Watson. 'As Elinor says, we are sane. Yet I, at least, will not leave this place. There are two dangerously mad men chained up in another part of these cellars and kept in the most appalling conditions. I will not leave them in the hands of this ignorant couple.'

'Ma'am,' began Flemynge, 'you can't wish to stay —'

'Oh, but I do! You are a wealthy man, sir, and I know you are a good one, because Elinor has told me so. Won't you consider buying Chennings? I would like very much to be in charge of just such an establishment, properly staffed, of course.'

McCann was not slow to see his chance. 'I'll sell you the house for a thousand pounds.'

'Five hundred,' said Flemynge.

'Done, sir. Now what are we to do?'

'I must leave this place as soon as possible,' I told Flemynge. 'There has been great sickness here and several people have died. I don't want to expose my child to the disease.'

Flemynge turned to Miss Watson, but she shook her head. 'I will not leave without the two male patients.'

I let out a long sigh and lifted my head from the comfort of my husband's chest. For the past half an hour I had known what I must do, what my life had been a preparation for.

'Flemynge, we will all go to Thorsby. Miss Watson and Mrs Porter will travel with us. Mr and Mrs McCann will take the two men in their own carriage and travel directly to the dower house where they will stay under our watchful eyes until Chennings has been altered and suitable staff taken on. When all is ready, Miss Watson and the men will return here and the McCanns may go on their way.'

'Elinor, my love, you won't want to be reminded –'

I closed his lips with my fingers. 'I can never forget. My life is inextricably entwined with the plight of the insane. It is my duty to do what I can for them. I confess I could never come to this place to work as Miss Watson wishes to do, but I cannot turn my back on my experiences and think no more about insanity. I will work from Thorsby. I will write about my time here. Using my knowledge and your money to improve the lot of the insane, I will try to ensure that no other sane person is ever sent to a madhouse for evil reasons.'

'A mammoth task,' said Flemynge. 'Self-interest will always cause a few people to convince themselves of a relative's insanity. And medical men know so little about the mind, that it will always be possible to fool some of them, no matter how the laws are strengthened. Nevertheless, your decision is a brave one.'

'No, I think it is probably quite cowardly. By involving myself with madhouses, I hope that I may never again be committed for the wrong reasons.'

'Elinor,' said Miss Watson, 'I, too, must confess to some confusion and error. I owe you an apology. I implied that you were insane to fight against your imprisonment the first time you came to Chennings. I suggested that to endure with fortitude was the only sane response to this great injustice. I was wrong. To be true to ourselves, we must oppose evil whenever the opportunity arises. Anger and struggle can save us from mental destruction. I wish, in a way, that I had tried to escape with you last night. One of us might have got away to raise the alarm.'

'But you were prevented from going because of your love for Mrs Porter and concern for the male patients, just as I was compelled to try to escape because of my love for Flemynge.'

Flemynge pushed the damp curls from my forehead. 'My love, you spoke of Thorsby. At this moment, I have the deeds to the Old Manor House in my pocket. After all the trouble I have been to, do you now tell me that you are prepared to live at Thorsby?'

I apologized for having put him to so much needless effort, admitting that I didn't want to live at the Old Manor House after all.

'That house belongs to my childhood,' I said. 'I wanted to leave Thorsby and return to being a carefree little girl in Gloucestershire. The last twenty-four hours have changed all that. Thorsby is my home. I intend to make everyone in Essex understand that we belong there and have come to stay.'

Within half an hour, Flemynge and Mr McCann had cleaned up the male patients, poor wretches, a frail old man with a white beard and confused eyes, and an emaciated fellow of about forty who possessed demonic strength. The two were chained hand and foot and secured inside the McCanns' carriage. Their bewilderment on seeing the beautiful autumn day and feeling the sharp breeze against their faces, was most moving. Small grey swifts darted and swooped low over the grounds, feeding as they flew. The old man laughed to see them, his spirit seemingly unbroken by all that he had suffered.

Flemynge said that he would write to Mr Tuke for advice immediately. No one, no matter how violent, was chained up at The Retreat. Other methods of restraint were used, but only when absolutely necessary. These two patients would be housed humanely but securely at the dower house and given fresh air and good food. Mr McCann smirked and gave his wife a knowing look, as if to say he knew that Flemynge was a fool, but I felt sure he was right.

The journey seemed to take for ever, but was enlivened by the pleasure Katherine and Mrs Porter took in all they saw after so many months spent within the walls of Chennings.

Finally, we entered the grounds of Thorsby and started down the long drive. I put my head out of the window to look at the graceful lines of the house, just as the sun broke through the racing clouds. The front door opened; out came Somers, Grimsby and Barlow, quickly followed by every indoor servant. The gardeners and stable staff came running, joined by tenants, their wives and children, all waving and cheering as we approached.

I turned to Flemynge, my heart too full for speech.

My husband took my hand and raised it to his lips. 'You are home, Elinor, home at last.'